Blood of The Lamb

Kaitlyn Smith

Blood of The Lamb

First printing, 2026

Printed in the United States of America

This is a work of fiction. The story, all names, character, and incidents portrayed in this production are fictitious. No identification with actual persons (living or deceased), places, buildings, and products is intended or should be referred.

Book Cover by: Miblart

ISBN: 979-8-218-93240-4

DEDICATION

For those who may be possessed or easily scared.

BLOOD OF THE LAMB

<u>One</u>

It's hot outside today. I closed my eyes as my face tilted toward the sky, letting the sun's rays wash over me like a shower. The sun traced burning lines around the skin it could reach, haloing me in a steady, uncomfortable warm light. Sweat pooled along my back and arms as small droplets traced the side of my head and down my chin. I could feel strands of my hair that escaped my braids laying against my temples and around my ears. The humidity settled around my skin in a heavy blanket which made the air feel thick as it sealed around me in a musky-wet embrace. Rustling to my right caught my ears, my eyes snapped open, scanning the line of trees. Nothing moved. I waited – watching.

My gaze trailed over the short, squat trees. Their slender trunks bent in odd shapes as their branches curled this way and that as if melting against the heat. Unlike most trees, these didn't seem too eager to reach for the sun. Their leaves were thin and small, bunching together in clusters providing little to no shade for the ground below. There wasn't much grass, the few sparse blades that did survive were yellowed and scorched. Everything seemed to be a dull dusty brown from lack of water. It made the world blend together. Dad called it 'brush country'. He said most of the south looked like this. I sighed. *He didn't say it would feel this hot though.*

My eyes trailed down the patchwork of grass, sand, and twigs that made up the ground until they landed in a divet. The dirt looked worn and tired as if someone had purposefully wallowed it out, hoping for some reprieve against the harsh sun and heat. Claw marks of various animals tracked through it, tearing away at the little tufts of grass that tried to take root there. It seemed to be the only area where the ground had been disturbed. It was the only bit of ground that deviated from the consistently flat, dead grass as far as the eye could see.

I began to take a step, but a sudden hard shove to my back made me falter and lose my balance. My hands flailed in front of me, desperate to brace for the fall. The world tilted and spun, rushing past in a rush of muted color. I landed in the divet I had been observing, dust floating and twirling in the air around me and in my lungs. My arms stung against the hard, dry ground. I coughed and squeezed my eyes shut.

"Watch it freak," A voice spat behind me, laughter filled the air from a few different voices. I coughed again sending another flurry of dust spiraling through the air. I blinked away tears, but my eyelids felt like gritty sandpaper against my eyes, making it worse.

"She's like a dog," A new voice this time. More laughter resounded. "Rolling around in the dirt because you have fleas."

I turned around. Three girls stood before me. I couldn't make out their faces very well due to the position of the sun, but I knew exactly who they were. I put my arm up to block the glaring light.

Squinting from both the light and dirt I coughed again before speaking. "Leave me alone." My voice was weak and hoarse. Their smiles grew wide.

"Your parents should take you to a groomer," The one with auburn hair, Autumn, said. Freckles adorned her rosy cheeks like mud splatter. Her white tank top and khaki shorts looked new. "That's where we take my dogs when they need a bath."

"Yeah, and it looks like you really need one," The blonde, Ivy, said next. Her red headband was bright against her hair. "You stink."

"Here why don't you play fetch?" The brunette, Lea, had picked up a stick the same color as her eyes and shirt.

Leave me alone.

"I throw it and you be a good doggy and go get it." I watched as she reeled her arm back, tossing the stick at the edge of the tree line. I didn't move.

"Well?" Autumn looked at me with a raised eyebrow. "Go get it."

"No." I responded. My fingers dug into the dense, hard ground forming cracks along the surface. Pushing past small rocks and dried out clay as dirt embedded itself under my nails, I felt small.

"Dogs don't speak," Ivy's eyes darkened. "They *bark*."

They started to move towards me, I backed away instinctively, crawling along the ground, the sharp, dead grass stinging my hands. My eyes looked around frantically, searching for anyone to help, but I couldn't see past them. Lea reached down and grabbed my shirt collar, hoisting me up to my knees, her face only inches from mine.

"Bad dogs get punished," Her voice was low, her brow furrowed. Tears began to fall along my cheeks, uncomfortable from the dust and sand. She raised an arm, blocking the sun with her hand, ready to strike. I was faster. As my hand let go of the dirt it had been clutching, she screamed. The dirt swirled in the air, settling into her hair and against her skin.

"Hey!" Ms. Vera yelled, as she drew closer Ivy let go of my collar. I sat on my heels. "What in the world is going on here?" Once she reached the four of us, she placed her fists on her hips, staring down at us, an eyebrow raised.

"We were just playing," Autumn responded in a fake, light tone, though there was a hint of aggravation in it. The other two nodded and smiled.

She turned to me. "Petra is that true?" I studied the other three for a moment. They watched me like a wolf watches a rabbit, waiting and hungry. They weren't scared of Ms. Vera, besides what could she possibly do?

"Yeah," I nodded. She paused, not seeming to believe me, the three gave her wide, toothy grins.

"Told ya," Lea laughed. Ms. Vera wrung her hands together, small pops resounding from the joints.

"Okay well run along then," She gave them a dismissive wave, watching them skip and laugh away to join our classmates on the playground. "Why don't you come with me? It's almost pick up time anyways." She reached out a hand. Her nails were painted a faint purple. She helped me up with little to no effort, not letting go of my hand, instead choosing to dust me off with her other. She looked at the palms of my hands, little, tiny cuts covering the surface as dirt clung to them.

"What do you say we go inside and get you cleaned up? No more throwing dirt, alright?" She said, a small reassuring smile spread across her lips.

"Yeah," I nodded. I watched her for a second as she walked, pulling me in tow, her eyes scanning the other kids crawling along the playground like ants. My hand looked small in hers, her purple, knit cardigan sleeve brushing gently against my wrist. A single thread hung loose, swaying slightly. We stopped by Mr. Taylor, a scrawny man in a brown suit with thin glasses and grey hair. He taught math on Wednesdays and science on Fridays. He was a nervous man, always talking fast and about things I didn't really understand, but sometimes he'd bring his telescope to school. Those were my favorite days.

Ms. Vera spoke a few muffled words to him while he nodded, a quick and jerky motion that made his thin grey hair sway violently.

He turned to me, his pale blue eyes wide. "Goodbye Petra, have a great weekend." He gave a small smile, his crooked, yellowed teeth stained from drinking far too much coffee. I smiled slightly but stopped when I noticed the three girls from the corner of my eye. They were watching me intently from the edge of the playground, their arms crossed and their faces scowling.

"Let's go," Ms. Vera tugged me in the opposite direction.

The trek to the classroom wasn't very long, mostly boring and quiet. The grass crunching beneath our feet was the loudest part. Once inside the air conditioning hit my skin like a brick, melting away at the humid blanket I had taken comfort in. I began to shiver, my muscles trembling against the sudden cold.

The school could barely hold its own against the giants I knew from before our move two years ago. It consisted of exactly one hallway that led to two classrooms, large windows lined the walls of the classrooms so you could see inside. Both rooms were capped at the end by a bathroom. Further forward on the right-hand side were doors to the admin like the principal, counselor, and other office people. Then the singular door on the left belonged to the nurse. At the end of the hallway were the doors to leave. I stared at them for a moment, the light wood stain darkened by the glow of light cascading through the tiny windows. They looked tired on their old, rusted hinges.

The jingling of keys brought my attention back to the rooms on either side of me. Both classrooms' lights were turned out; everyone was on the playground for the last hour before our parents came. The stark white of the walls barely a light grey as the windows allowed light to pour in.

The dirt on my shoes stood out distinctly against the white, grey-speckled tiles. Ms. Vera continued to fiddle with the keys on her lanyard around her neck until she managed to find the right one and unlock the door. With a swift flick of her hand, the lights buzzed alive, drowning the room in an awful flickering white.

"Here," She pushed books to the side of her desk. "Come sit up here." She patted the now empty spot on the desk with her hand, the sound reverberating through the empty room. She fiddled with a drawer at her filing cabinet to the left, I turned, letting my eyes drift.

The entire place smelled like warm vanilla and honey. It was sickly sweet, coating my mind in a headache of sugar. Four rows of five small desks sat in the center of the room. They were made of pale wood and rusted metal, some half broken and chipped. Two bookshelves adorned with small fake plants in colorful pots, stuffed animals, and tons of books sat at the very back of the classroom, a tiny purple rug in front of them. On the right-hand wall, underneath the windows, was the calendar and assignment cubby, where we turned in all our homework. Our names each sat above their own cubby written in sharpie on a piece of masking tape. To the left stood a single computer. It looked old and worn, more like an old TV than a computer. My dad's computer looked nothing like this one. It was boxy and sounded like an engine when you turned it on. Ms. Vera had hung purple letters spelling out 'workstation' above it. I'd never seen anyone use the computer besides her, but she said one day someone would. A lone window sat above it, casting in the daylight, but the golden rays were suffocated by the bright white lights overhead.

"Here we go," I turned back to my teacher. She held a dry white rag and bottle of water, quickly opening it and pouring it over the rag. "Let me see."

Her hand was soft as she held my chin, gently dragging the rough and damp rag across my face. Each time she pulled it away the white became a muddier muted brown. She pulled at my hands next, unfurling them and mopping up the dirt, even going so far as to clean under my nails. Her mousy brown hair fell from her ponytail to frame her face. Small strands of hair tussled and curled around her ears having also escaped. Her cheeks were a slight rosy color, likely from the heat. She had a small nose and big eyes, like a mouse.

"There," She smiled at me, tucking a strand of hair behind my ear. "How's that?"

"Fine." I shrugged.

"Okay, well your dad will be here in a sec-"
"Already here," My eyes snapped to the door where he stood.

Dad was a tall man, his head nearing the top of the door frame. He still wore his white coat, his name plate glinting in the dim light. His brown hair was tussled as if he'd run his hand through it a million times. Dark circles lined his under eyes. He met my gaze as he smiled, showing perfect white teeth.

"Oh good!" Ms. Vera chuckled, putting the rag down and wiping her hands on her shirt and pants. She tried to smooth her hair along her ponytail but it didn't help much. "You're a bit early."

Dad ran his hand through his hair for the millionth and one time before reaching out his hand. "Yeah, I figured I'd pick her up a little early and get back to work." Their hands lingered for a moment. Ms. Vera put a second hand on top of both of theirs as she took in a breath.

"No rest for you lately, huh?" She pulled her hands away. He shook his head.

"You know me," He winked. "Always busy." They both laughed, the sound intertwining and echoing through the empty room.

"That's very true," She nervously wrung her hands.

"I hope she hasn't been giving you too much trouble," Dad looked over her shoulder at me, raising an eyebrow in question.

"No, no, of course not!" She laughed as she spoke, waving her hands wide in dismissal. "She's one of my best students."

There was an awkward pause as Dad nodded.

"Well anyway, I guess I should get her home seeing as my second shift starts in a few." He checked his watch casually, not really looking at the time. I slid off the desk, my feet hitting the tile with a hollow *thump*.

He watched me for a second before turning back to Ms. Vera. "I'll see you soon."

I grabbed my backpack from my desk before heading to the door.

"Have a great weekend guys," Ms. Vera waved us goodbye. Their eyes lingered on each other for a moment as we left, Dad not turning away until we were nearly out of sight.

The walk to the car was mostly silent, but the car ride back was even worse. The silence felt suffocating, and my throat was dry. Dad didn't speak a word, preferring to remain in the silence of the drive, the only sound being the wind rushing through the slight crack of the windows.

Dad rarely ever turned the radio on, maybe it was because he was always so busy at the hospital or maybe it was all the noise of rushing nurses and screaming patients. If I were him, I'd want to sit in silence too, even if it were only for a few minutes.

I put my forehead against the glass; it was cold compared to outside. The scenery rushed past in a blur of muted color. Everything looked dry outside, like if you went to touch it, it would just crumble into a pile of dust.

The streets were mostly empty, save for a few cars here and there that would idle by. Where we lived was a small, sleepy town. There wasn't much to do here besides go to the movies or niche shops downtown. The rest was nothing but fields and fields of crops and cows. Corn, beans, cabbage, anything really. The town's main source of income came from their ability to grow and produce through farms, but due to the lack of available land to develop, it didn't grow in population. No one wanted to move here--except for my mom.

Two

My backpack hit the hardwood floor with a hallow *thud*. The books inside causing the bag to slump over, deflating as it collapsed. The hallow sound of approaching footsteps resounded to my left.

Mom came around the corner from the kitchen, her eyes lighting up.

"Mom!" I ran to hug her.

"There's my girl," She embraced me tightly, squeezing me as hard as she could. "How was school?"

She pushed me away, her hands gripping my shoulders. She sat eye level with me, her light green eyes focused intently on mine. Faint freckles splattered across her cheeks and nose. Her skin was tanned from years under the sun, her eyelids forming crows' feet at the corners when she smiled. Her dark auburn hair was pulled into a low ponytail, small, frizzy curls pointing every which way.

"I have to go," Dad said dryly. Mom looked up, blinking quickly as she watched him by the door.

Mom stood, her right hand moving to the top of my head. "Oh, you have a second shift today?"

Dad merely took a quick glance at her before nodding and turning towards the door. "I'll be home late so don't wait up." And with that he was gone. The slight slam of the old wooden door was loud against my ears. I looked to Mom.

Her face was calm as she sat perfectly still. Her body tense and rigid, her jaw locked tight as she pursed her lips. Her eyes lingered on the door for a few more seconds until she suddenly snapped out of it.

"Alright, well who needs a stinky boy around anyways?" She turned to me with a smile. Mom's teeth were crooked, but a comforting kind of crooked. I think it made her smile prettier. "I have a big surprise outside."

"What is it?" I asked.

"I'm not entirely sure yet." Excitement lit up her features, her eyes wide. I gave her a confused look.

"Then how is it a surprise?" I asked.

"Well, it's still underground," She placed her hands on her knees, drawing her face closer to mine. "You want to help me dig it up?" She raised an eyebrow, seeming to hold her breath as she waited for my response.

"Sure," I nodded. I didn't really want to.

"Great!" She exclaimed. "Put your bag up and let's get to work." She ruffled my hair as she turned. I picked up my bag before heading for the stairs.

Our house was old. Its hardwood floors were dark and stained with the weight of age. To the left of the entrance lay the kitchen and dining rooms, both worn. To the right is the laundry room, always humming faintly, the smell of freshly dried clothes clinging to the air. Past that was the living room, with its single sagging leather couch and steady glow of the large flat-screen TV. But straight ahead, framed in shadow, rose the staircase to the second floor.

I clambered up the stairs in a hurry, the dull echo of my footsteps trailing behind me. Once at the landing, the upstairs felt much smaller than the floor below. Directly ahead was my bathroom, to the right, my parents' room and the spare room across from it. The door to their room hung open, but the darkness inside hid everything from view. My own room was to the left, with the spare bedroom just opposite mine. Old boxes collecting dust, filled with small trinkets and books sat against the wall by my door. Mom has been saying she'd eventually unpack them for a year now, but I don't think she'll get to them anytime soon.

Once in my room I took a breath. *I'm tired.* My mind and body felt sluggish. It felt as if my bones themselves just wanted to pile onto my bed and stay there forever. The walls of my room were a deep green, books and countless posters covered the wall to my left. A small dresser sat by itself against the wall. My bed, with a leaf print comforter, sat in the middle of the back wall to my right covered in stuffed animals. A large window to its right, letting light flood through the room and spill across the floor. Straight ahead was my closet, ricket old, slatted doors harboring the mess inside.

I tossed my bag on the ground by my bed, taking a second to peer through the window. The view overlooked a small fenced in area by the back shed where the sheep were kept. Sometimes I liked to sit and watch them playing when the weather was nice. One of the sheep was noticeably larger than the others. Mom said she was due to have a baby soon. I smiled.

"Petra, come on we're losing daylight," Mom called up.

I ran back down the stairs, my quick footsteps loud through the house.

Mom walked fast. Her stride was triple the size of mine. She kept the brisk pace, never slowing, her eyes focused solely in front of her, only looking back periodically to make sure I was keeping up.

Sweat clung to my lower back and forehead. The air was heavy, weighing down my arms and legs like a thick blanket. My lungs stung a bit from the effort to keep up, my legs burning as we trudged through the woods behind our house.

"Just over here," Mom moved a few branches out of her way, showing a small clearing ahead. "Watch your step."

Upon entering the clearing my breath hitched. A rectangular patch of soil had been carefully carved nearly six feet down in the center of the clearing, the green grass giving way to cliffs of sheared and perfectly removed dirt. Tools were strewn about the place. Clear containers lay stacked in the sun, each one labeled with a date and identifying numbers.

Stepping closer to the clearing my brow furrowed. Mom had painstaking dug in a grid pattern. Each grid was a two foot by two-foot square. Due to her digging pattern each square was lower than the last as they circled toward the center.

I watched as her thin frame climbed down on one side, her feet hitting the earth with a solid *thud*. She held her arms out towards the edge, she was only about four feet in, closer to the shallow end of the hole.

"Sit on the edge and push off," She waved her hands at me. I did as she said. Mom placed her hands under my armpits and as I pushed away from the wall of dirt, she hoisted me down gently.

"Here," She handed me a spade. "You'll take this square here." She pushed me along, pointing at a small, upturned patch of dirt. It looked dry.

"Do I-"

She cut me off. "Just dig sweetheart," She gave a reassuring smile. "I'll be right next to you."

I watched as her eyes scoured the grids around mine. "The metal detector was going off like crazy around here earlier." She mumbled.

As I crouched the smell of soggy soil and broken grass perforated the air. I pushed the spade into the ground, watching as it sunk into the earth before pulling out a small mound of dirt. The little mound didn't seem to be worth much to me, but Mom had set a container down between us with a fresh label.

"What do you think is down here?" I asked as I placed another pile of dirt into the container.

"I'm not sure," She shook her head. "That's why it's a surprise."

My gaze moved to observe her for a second. She moved with careful speed as she worked. Her spade seemed almost surgical as it dug perfect lines into the ground.

The silence began to grow as I turned back to my patch of dirt. She took a breath before continuing.

"Apparently, a long time ago there was a cult that performed rituals in this area. They were nomadic and travelled all across the country, but from some of the logs I've read this was the last place they were recorded at."

She wiped at her brow.

"A cult?" I asked.

"Yeah," She stopped for a second, pondering. "A religious group. I've been following them around the country trying to trace their origins and uncover their full story. They're what I'm writing my book on."

"So, like a church?" I pushed at the ground with my spade, watching the way the dirt crumbled. Mom laughed, the sound echoing through the trees.

"Kind of," She nodded. "But in more of an evil kind of way."

I stopped digging, "What makes them evil?"

"They do bad things, like sacrifice, manipulate, exploit and often times abuse their people."

"Oh," I turned back to my dirt laden spade, watching my muddied reflection try to stare back.

"How was school?" Mom asked.

I stopped digging, my eyes searching the ground. I wasn't sure how to answer.

School sucks. It's the worst.

I clenched my jaw, stabbing further and further into the ground with the spade. Anger fueling the movements as I dug. I wanted to crawl into the ground and lay there. *I don't want to go back.*

I shoved the spade into the dirt until my fingers were engulfed in it. The cold of the soil made my fingers feel numb. Tears pricked at the back of my eyes. *I'd rather die.*

"Sweetheart?" I looked up. Mom had stopped digging, a worried look scrawled across her features.

"School is fine," Though I shrugged, my voice waivered. Mom watched me for a few minutes like she watched Dad leaving earlier, quiet and unmoving.

"You promise?" Her voice was soft. "You know you can tell me anything, right?" She continued to dig, no longer looking at me.

I turned to face the sky. The trees around us were still squat and twisted, the same as those at the school. At least these ones had green leaves to contrast the dull grey of their bark. The limbs danced gently in the breeze, creating a soft ruffling sound as they touched. I took a deep breath, closing my eyes for a second to gather my courage. A lump formed in my throat. *She'll understand.*

"Mom, I-"

"Wait! Look! Look!" She yelled excitedly. I moved closer to her, looking down into the area she had been digging through. A glint of gold peaked out from the ground. She moved the spade away, pushing the dirt aside with her hands in her excitement. "This is incredible." She breathed.

She continued to brush away at the dirt, a large disc of gold slowly being unearthed. The disc had a design carved into the center, the top edge lined with foliage. In the center sat the head of a lion, three horse legs and three goat legs surrounded it in a weird display.

As I watched her uncover more and more of the golden disc my stomach began to feel uneasy. My skin felt cold, even in the gross humid heat. I swallowed, my throat felt dry.

"Amazing," She placed a hand under the edge of it gently tugging at it away from the ground. "Ow! Shit!"

She dropped the disc, holding the pointer finger of her right hand.

"What happened?" I asked.

"I just pricked my finger," She held up her hand, a small drop of blood collecting on the tip of her finger. "Nothing to worry about."

I watched the blood pool and fall. The droplet spun in the air, turning and twisting upon itself until it fell against the golden metal. It stained the surface, bright even against the glint of the sun. I watched as the blood sunk into the crevices of the carving, sinking into the face of the lion, pooling in the depths of its eyes as if it were crying.

"Oh no," Mom picked the metal back up quickly, wiping at the blood.

My gaze fell to where she had removed the golden disc from. Several rows of flowers sat in the ground, all bunched together, their stems wrapped individually in twine. The edges of the twine had frayed and broken apart showing the thorns along the flower stems. Teeth and other small bones decorated in odd engravings were laced with twine also, hiding in between the edges of the flowers, filling in the gaps. The flowers looked dried and old, but still oddly intact. *They didn't decompose?*

"Mom," Old pieces of paper lay just under the pile of flowers and bones. Wax seals with weird symbols kept them wrapped together.

"Wow," She continued to ogle the metal in her hands. It was larger than her palm and looked to be maybe a centimeter thick. The edge was smooth, glinting in the light as she turned it around in her hands. "This is amazing. Do you know what this is?"

"No," I replied honestly.

"This looks to be a medallion of some sort," She studied it carefully. "Maybe used in ritualistic practices? Maybe blessings of some sort? With the carvings I can imagine maybe a shepherds blessing?"

She held the medallion out to me. The wind stirred, the trees grew loud as their branches smacked into one another. I felt my stomach churn. I

I shook my head.

"What do you think?" Mom asked, still offering it to me.

"I don't like it," I replied. She laughed, pulling the medallion back towards her before wrapping it carefully in linen.

"That's okay," She grabbed her camera. "Smile."

The corners of my lips tugged upwards slightly, unease crept along my skin as the camera flashed.

I watched as my fork pushed at the food on my plate. Salmon and broccoli. It smelled good, but for some reason I wasn't hungry. My throat felt scratchy and my stomach still felt queasy.

I shivered against the air conditioning, listening to it humming through the vents. My fork clinked slightly against the plate, organizing the broccoli pieces by size. Mom sat on the opposite side of the table. A magnifying glass clamped to it. She stared through it as she studied the medallion, its golden surface gleaming. Her hands trembled slightly as she turned it over, her gloves catching on the ornate hooves.

"It's incredibly detailed," Mom said as she turned to her laptop. Her chin tilted slightly up as her glasses sat at the end of her nose. Due to the humidity her hair had become frizzy, the pieces that poked out of her ponytail looking more disheveled. She typed a few words, the dull sound of the keys resounding as her fingers moved with precision.

I set down my fork, letting out a tired sigh. "When is Dad going to be home?"

Mom turned to me, her eyes lingering on the laptop screen for as long as they could. She paused for a brief moment.

"I'm not sure," She replied. I sighed again, pushing at the salmon now. She watched me for a second, pursing her lips.

"Can I have ice cream?" I asked.

"Not unless you finish your dinner," She turned back to her laptop. The keys clicked away.

"I don't like salmon," I mumbled under my breath. She stopped. Her gaze flicked between me and the plate.

"Eat half the broccoli and I can make you a PB&J?" She raised an eyebrow. A small smile tugged at the corner of my mouth. My eyes fell on the plate. The charred bits of roasted broccoli and bright orange salmon stared back at me. My stomach growled.

"Deal," I began to scoop up the pieces of broccoli, shoveling them into my mouth as quickly as I could. Mom smiled before standing.

"Do you think you'll eat the salmon tomorrow?" She called from the kitchen.

"I don't think so," I shook my head. The bland taste of broccoli filling my mouth as they crunched between my teeth.

"That's okay, your dad can eat it for lunch then," She came back to the table, a sandwich in one hand and a container in the other. "All good?"

I nodded as she took the plate away. With one quick motion the salmon was plopped into the container with the rest of the broccoli. It almost looked like the containers full of dirt she had back at the clearing.

I bit into the sandwich, relishing the sweet flavors that spread across my tongue. Mom sat back down at the end of the table, her knees popping as she winced.

She didn't put her gloves back on this time, instead picking up the medallion with her bare hand. She placed her chin on her other hand holding the medallion up to the light as her eyes traced over it.

"It's quite beautiful," Mom said as she turned it over in her hand, the metal sliding through her fingers.

My stomach churned, my skin growing cold. I felt the twisted hands of anxiety weave their way through my throat. The longer I stared at it the more uneasy I felt. Something burned in my chest and my bones trembled. Something felt deeply wrong.

Mom began to hum, a slow tune she was making up along the way. Her head tilted to the side as she studied the old artifact. My lungs burned as I held my breath. Tears pricked the back of my eyes. I wanted to get rid of it. To throw it back into the hole she dug it out of. To never see it again. *But why?*

My brow furrowed. *Why?* My mind swam as I stared, the edges of my vision growing dark, my ears ringing. Fear coiled its way around my chest, squeezing my lungs shut. *Why-*

BAM!

I jumped. My heart leapt to my throat. Mom let go of the medallion, startled. It clanged against the table before falling to the floor. It rolled in a lazy circle until it fell, the lion's head staring at us. We both looked at each other. Mom blinked a few times before turning to the window of the kitchen to her left. My gaze followed hers.

There was a large splatter of red fluid against the window. Inky, black feathers clung to it as others fell slowly, trailing down the glass.

My heart hammered in my ears, adrenaline shook my hands. My blood felt like ice.

"Must've been a bird," Mom stood, picking up the medallion and inspecting it for damage.

"Why would it do that?" I asked, my voice slipped against the lump in my throat.

"I don't know," She glanced at the window. "Maybe it got confused by the reflection. I'll go check it out." She placed the medallion at the edge of the table before heading for the door.

I stared at it for a moment. The lion's empty eyes almost seemed to stare back, waiting. The uneasy feeling began to slowly drape over me again. My chest began to burn as I held my breath once more. Fear pulled at my body, my lip quivering.

There was a ticking sound, then suddenly the legs that surrounded the lion began to move. The movement was jerky. I watched in terror as the legs continued lurching in a clockwise direction until one of the legs hung over the lion's head.

I felt my heartbeat quicken, my hands trembling as a cold sweat began to break out over my forehead. I rubbed my eyes, but the medallion remained. The lion stared back.

I jumped down from my chair, bolting for the door. *I need to get away.* Flinging the door open in a hurry I ran.

Before I could get far, I slammed into a wall, falling back onto the ground.

"Petra be careful," It wasn't a wall, it was Mom. "What're you doing running out like that?"

She bent down to help me up, brushing the dirt off my pants. I took a few deep breaths, trying to calm down.

"Petra what's wrong?" Mom asked, a worried look furrowed her brows.

I shook my head. "Nothing." She pursed her lips at my response. *It couldn't have been real.*

"Okay," She stood, turning back to head toward where the bird collapsed. I followed.

It was a small crow, not even fully grown. Its feathers were a mess. Strewn and broken, sharp shards of white bone sticking out between the joints. Dark red blood stained its broken and withered body. Its head was bent at an upturned and crooked angle. Its eye was still open, staring directly at us.

"Can we bury it?" I asked, sorrow filled my voice.

"Yeah, sure," Mom said as she nodded.

The hole was shallow and small. We had decided to bury it under the tree by the fence where the sheep stayed. Mom used the shovel to place the bird in the hole, before gently covering it with dirt. Once she finished she wiped at her brow.

"Do you want to say anything?" She asked as she turned to me.

"What?" I said puzzled.

She sucked in a breath. "Well normally at funerals people will say something nice about the person. I know a bird isn't a human, but it was once alive all the same, right?"

I nodded, taking a moment to think of what to say. The evening sun was slowly fading behind the trees, spilling beautiful shades of orange and yellow across the sky. The tree's shadows had grown long and twisted falling over the ground and smearing together. A breeze fell through the trees, swaying their branches. The sheep bayed behind us, calling to one another. The tinkling of the windchime on our front door made its way through the air to us.

"I hope you get to see mountains of bird seed wherever you are now," I said aloud, my voice soft against the wind.

"May your spirit rest undisturbed," Mom said next. She gave me a small smile. "Let's get back inside before it gets too late."

<u>Four</u>

My eyes trailed along the ceiling. The ridges and bumps that filled it almost looked like mountains, as if the ceiling was its own little piece of land. The shadows created by my nightlight pooled around the edges of the room. They stretched long and ugly, folding around each other like a cage. The ceiling fan spun, whirring in lazy circles. I sighed.

I looked at the door, muffled voices pouring from the hallway. My eyes glanced at the dinosaur plush in my arms. Its vacant green eyes stared back at me.

I pushed my way out from under the covers, my feet landing softly on the cold hardwood. My stomach churned as I neared the door, the voices growing louder. My hand reached up, twisting the knob before pushing the door open just enough to see through.

Warm orange light spilled out along the hallway from my parents' room. The door was wide open, hanging on its hinges in quiet silence. Shadows encased the stairs. I felt a shiver run along my spine.

"You've got to be kidding me," Dad's voice carried along the hall.

"I just want to know where you were," Mom this time, her voice sounded desperate.

"I already told you how many times?" I could hear the frustration in his voice.

"You said you had a second shift but-"

"So, I had a second shift, why is that so hard for you to believe?" Dad cut her off. There was a pause and then a loud sigh.

"I just don't remember you telling me," Mom spoke softer this time, her voice barely carrying.

"It's not my fault that your brain fails to remember shit," Dad grumbled.

There was another pause as silence filled the gaps between conversation. The tension was palpable, like this heavy weight along the air. It felt like humidity but sharper, digging into my skin and the marrow of my bones.

"A bird flew into the kitchen window today during dinner," Mom's voice was low.

"What?" Dad asked.

"A bird flew-"

"I heard you the first time," Dad cut her off again, huffing. "I was just…never mind."

"Petra and I buried it under the tree out back," Mom said. "She-"

"Wait, hold on," Dad interjected once again. "You let our eleven-year-old look at and handle a dead bird?"

"Well-no-it wasn't-I-" Mom stammered.

"Oh my god," The words sounded sharp against his tongue. "Are you fucking kidding me?"

"What?" Mom said, equally as frustrated.

"This is what I'm talking about," Dad stormed into the hallway, Mom following close behind.

"What are you going on about now?" She put a hand to her forehead.

"You don't think do you?" Dad put two fingers to his temple. "Hello? Earth to Terra, are you fucking stupid?"

Mom visibly recoiled, a look of pain scuttled across her face. Dad shook his head in disgust.

"It wasn't that big of a deal," She mumbled under her breath, rolling her eyes.

"It wasn't that big of a deal?" Dad mocked. "Really? That thing was probably diseased-"

"It was not! It likely ran into the window because it was confused-"

"Confused? Like you are right now?" Dad took a step towards her, and she instinctively stepped back. "I swear to god you have no brains."

Mom began to cough. The sound wracked her lungs, pulling the air from her throat in a scratchy noise. Dad pulled back.

"Diseased," He spat. "Just like I said. Now you probably have bird flu or something."

Mom looked at him with tired eyes, the coughing subsided. "Oh yeah? Is that your official doctor's diagnosis?" She rolled her eyes.

"Yeah, so what if it is?" Dad scoffed.

"Humans can't get bird flu, get a grip," She hissed.

"Humans have gotten bird flu before, you're not special," He looked at her incredulously.

"On the rare occasion. I didn't even touch the damn thing," She began to cough again.

For the briefest second Dad looked concerned, but it faded just as quickly as it appeared.

"You were stupid enough to let our daughter see it," Dad shook his head. "So maybe you're stupid enough to contract whatever disease it died from."

I watched as Mom seemed to shrink, folding in on herself and tucking parts of her away. She tugged at her robe and wrung her hands before crossing her arms.

"Why don't you sleep in here tonight?" She motioned toward their bedroom door, giving a forlorn glance at the empty room before meeting his gaze.

Dad sighed. His shoulders pulled down as if a weight had been placed on them. "No, I don't want to be around you right now. Especially not with that cough, I can't afford to be sick."

Mom looked hurt. "We haven't slept in the same bed in months."

"And?" Dad shrugged, his eyes staring past her.

Mom's jaw clenched, her body going rigid. Her eyes burned, boring into him. Dad looked uncomfortable against her stare.

"Okay, if you change your mind the door will be open." With that she turned and headed for their bedroom. Dad stayed in the hallway watching. The anger that had so suddenly inflated his chest, died. His lungs fell and his muscles looked weak. It was as if he were a balloon, and his entire body deflated. He pinched the bridge of his nose, letting out a tired sigh. He stared for a few more seconds, his eyes lingering at the doorway for a moment until the lights flicked off. The warm yellow glow no longer illuminated the hallway. Instead, the cold blue of the moonlight through the window to his right washed over him. He ran a hand through his hair before heading to the spare bedroom. The door shut with a quiet *thump*.

I stared at the empty hallway. My heart felt numb, and my throat held a lump in it.

"Mom's not stupid," The words caught in my throat, but instead of carrying, it barely slipped between the crack of my door, dying before it ever got close to their ears. I wish my voice would carry. I wish Dad would hear it. I wish Mom would hear it. But they wouldn't. It didn't matter.

They did that most nights. Arguing as if I couldn't hear them. I watched them fight each time. I could feel it. The tension and the sickness that had grown between their hearts was almost visible at this point. They barely talked during the day. I don't even remember the last time they hugged or kissed one another.

We never should have moved. That was when everything changed. Dad was upset he had to leave his old hospital, even though mom told him to stay. He complained about it a lot the first few weeks, then it stopped. Suddenly Dad was working longer hours and picking up extra shifts. It was like he didn't want to be home, like he didn't want to see us.

Mom wanted to move here for work. She told Dad if he didn't want to move with, it was okay, she'd only be at this site for a few years. But Dad wasn't having it. He didn't like that she was always travelling.

He especially didn't like Mom's boss, Dan. He would travel with Mom sometimes and that made Dad extra angry. He'd get really mean those days.

I crawled my way back under the covers, holding the stuffed dinosaur close to my chest. I put my forehead to it. *We never should have moved.*

It was hard to sleep. My body tossed and turned as my mind struggled to relax. It was cold in the house, but no matter how many blankets I had over me it didn't feel like enough. The moon hung just at the edge of the top of my window, gazing down at me intently. I let out a frustrated sigh.

My mind buzzed with nothing and everything at the same time. It felt like static pooling in the depths of my skull. I was stuck in an infinite loop of thought and there was no way out. *I'm drowning.*

My eyes snapped open. The cool light of my nightlight greeting me. Shadows filled the room like long overgrown tendrils of weeds. They twisted over each other before they smothered themselves in every corner of the room. I waited.

Nothing happened for a few minutes, but then, there it was. The sound of scratching at my door. It was soft, close to the bottom. I tilted my head to the left, letting my eyes trail along the darkness until they rested on the bottom of the door. I held my breath.

And there it was again. Unmistakable. It only lasted a few seconds. Just three small scratches back and forth against the wood grain, before it would stop. I felt my heartbeat quicken. *Theres nothing there.*

My gaze floated to the crack underneath the door, watching the darkness that laid beyond. There was a small movement, the light from my room spilling over feet shrouded in shadow. My eyes widened, my blood running cold.

I stood, careful to be quiet. The sound of my bed creaking was loud against the quiet of the room. I clutched my dinosaur plush to me until my knuckles turned white. My stomach tossed and turned, dread filling the very core of my being, shaking my bones.

As I tiptoed to the door my heart began to slam into my chest. It hammered against my ribs begging to be released. My mind swirled and filled, the static growing louder. I stopped, inches from the door.

Muffled wheezes filled the silence. I couldn't hear them from my bed, but now, so close to the door I could. Tired, labored breathing sent through a scratchy and hoarse throat. I almost leapt from my skin as the scratches ensued, this time a bit louder, rougher.

I slowly got on my hands and knees, pushing my hair out of my eyes. I peered under the door, trying to see anything through the dark.

My heart leapt to my throat. An eye stared back at me, the rest of their face hidden behind the door. Their hair matted and tangled against the floor. I reeled back, crawling across the ground, my fingers grabbing at everything and nothing.

They began to pound on the door, rattling it on its hinges. I felt tears rolling down my cheeks. The banging was loud, incessantly filling my ears like a disgusting drum. The doorknob spun, twisting as the door swung open.

I felt a scream rip from my throat, tearing at my lungs as I pushed myself against the side of my bed, trying desperately to get away.

"Petra!" I opened my eyes, the lights bright against them. Mom crouched next to me, Dad standing in the doorway. Both looked troubled.

"What happened?" Mom asked. Her and Dad exchanged a quick glance.

"It was probably a bad dream, right?" Dad asked. I took a few shuddering breaths. My hands trembled. *Was it?*

"Yeah," I replied, uncertain. Unease crept along my skin, its cold fingers trailing the outline of my body. I shivered.

"Here, why don't we get you back into bed?" Mom stood, helping me up and moving the covers aside. I gulped. Dad came over to help tuck me in.

"Better?" Dad asked.

"Yeah," I lied. I couldn't shake the feeling.

"Okay well, get some rest now," Mom kissed the top of my head, smoothing my hair away from my forehead. "If you need either of us you know where we are."

"Goodnight," Dad headed for the door first, turning back at the doorway to give me a tired, but worried glance.

Mom's eyes lingered for a bit as she left. She turned the lights out as she closed the door.

The image from earlier seared into my mind. Every time I closed my eyes it stared back, so I kept them open. If I closed my eyes for more than a few seconds, my pulse would hammer through my veins and force me awake. Fear sat on my chest like an anvil, heavy and unwanted.

As time passed and the moon began to dip below the silhouette of the trees, my eyes grew heavy. They slowly fell, the static in my mind slowing to empty white space, my pulse slowing to a crawl. I could feel sleep's arms pulling me deeper into my mattress, tugging me free from the fear that slept next to me. As I began to drift my body felt weightless. *Finally.*

I shot up, my eyes snapped open, my pulse thrummed in my ears. The scratching noise pierced my ears once more. I turned slowly to face the door. My breath hitched at the site of the shadow covered feet. Terror drug me by the throat under my covers. *If I hide, it won't see me.*

This time the scratches didn't stop after a few seconds. Instead, they continued, itching away at the delicate wood like a fervent animal. I squeezed my eyes shut, clawing at my comforter. The scratching grew louder, more intense, pushing at the door so it would clack against the door jamb. The sound of the wood slamming together grew faster and more aggressive. The muffled sounds of wheezing, labored breathing poured over the noise.

Please. Sobs racked my body as snot and tears mixed along my sheets and face.

I hugged my dinosaur tighter, but the scratching and slamming only grew louder, the wheezing drawing closer.

Please stop. I begged.

And then it did.

Five

I stared at the table. The grain of the wood mimicking that of my door. Its delicate patterns pushed and pulled at one another, twisting but never touching. Each line looked like its own individual river, cutting through the wood with ease.

My gaze moved up slowly following the small path carved out in front of me. Then they landed on it. The lion's eyes stared back, haunting. The leg from last night still sat above its head. My eyes felt heavy, but they refused to shut. Fear tugged at the marrow in my bones and dread chilled my veins.

I placed a hand to the table, feeling the grooves beneath my fingertips. I let my pointer finger sway back and forth, slowly then faster, digging my nail into the clear coat.

"Hey! Stop that," Mom stood over me, placing a bowl of cereal on the table. "You're going to ruin it."

Her hand brushed along where my nail had traced. *The noise wasn't the same.* Her brow furrowed as her eyes connected with the medallion opposite me. *Maybe I imagined it.*

"That's strange," She said.

I perked up, watching as she picked up the piece of metal. She turned it over in her hands, observing the carving, biting at her lip. She ran a thumb over the carving, but suddenly stopped, a coughing fit clawing at her lungs. She set it down and rushed to the kitchen. I could hear the clinking of glass and then the sink being turned on. The coughing stopped.

"Are you sick?" I asked.

"Maybe," I gave a worried glance to her response. She shook her head. "I'm sure it's nothing."

She took a few more gulps of water. She looked exhausted. Her hair was unkempt and unbrushed. It sat in a low bun against the back of her neck. She hadn't cleaned the smudges of makeup left over around her eyes. Mom was an early riser, always dressed and ready for the day in her usual fashion of jeans and button down, but today she wore her grey sweats and a large black T-shirt. A slight red tint coated her under eyes and cheeks. She took a breath, putting the back of her hand to her forehead.

"Well, I don't have a fever," She gave a reassuring smile. Her teeth were a dull, foul yellow. "Eat your breakfast so we can go run our errands for today." She waved a dismissing hand to me.

I turned to look at the window. The spatters of blood and other bodily fluids from the bird remained. It had dried, stuck and flaking. The breeze gently tugged at the feathers that still persisted against the glass. The morning sun sat barely over the short trees. Everything looked greyer and more monotonous than usual. As if the muted colors of the brush country somehow diminished even more.

My eyes flitted to the cereal. It had turned soggy by now. Many of the pieces had sunk to the bottom. I stirred the spoon around, watching the way the cereal followed its path. The thought of eating made me want to puke.

"Honey, are you not hungry?" Mom patted my head, letting her fingers trail down through my hair. "You okay?"

I nodded. "Just tired."

Mom made a pouty face, sticking out her lip. "Aw, well you don't have to go run errands with me then. You can stay home and rest."

My eyes moved to the medallion, tracing its cold metallic surface.

"No, I want to go," I stood from the table quickly, scurrying upstairs to finish getting ready.

We lived just on the outskirts of the city, far enough away that homes were separated by several acres and wooded lots, but close enough it didn't take long to reach downtown. The town square encircled the courthouse. Its large white stone stained with decades of erosion, rain, and graffiti. Large streaks of rust and dirt pooled down the sides and swaths of color peaked out from the poor paint jobs done to hide them.

The buildings surrounding the courthouse were rustic. Their dilapidated nature providing some sort of 'southern charm' Mom had said. Each one of the buildings was made of the same red bricks. Some shops had taken to painting over them, others keeping the natural look. Most of the shops had awnings of various heights shading their small portion of the sidewalk. Signs of different colors and lights shined in the blistering afternoon sun. The decorative exterior moulding along each of the buildings provided a traditional feel. It felt like stepping back in time.

People walked along the sidewalk and weaved between the parallel parked cars, holding drinks in hand. Sweat beaded along their cups, the heat melting the ice almost immediately. The sounds of laughter and conversation floated through the cracked window of the passenger side of Mom's truck.

A coughing fit erupted from Mom's lungs. The sound was ragged and wet, as if her lungs were filled with water. She took a few breaths, closing her eyes and putting a hand to her forehead.

She sighed heavily, looking at me through the rearview mirror. "Alright, let's get these errands done and get home so we can watch a movie. How does that sound?" She gave a small smile. The bags under her eyes looked darker than this morning.

"Sounds good to me," I replied.

Stepping out of the truck into the sweltering heat was the worst. The heat from the sun bounced up from the pavement in wavy lines. When the breeze fell along the ground it only pushed the hot air closer to your body. The humidity felt sticky and gross. My mood felt immediately sour.

Mom came around the truck, reaching for my hand as she headed for the grocery store.

The smell of mildew and mold enveloped the entirety of the store. Bright white, fluorescent lights glared against the semi-white metal shelves. The shelves were barely stocked. There was only a handful of each product sitting on the shelves, collecting dust. Soft elevator music sung from the speakers. It felt surreal.

"We just need to grab a few quick things," Mom grabbed a basket before coughing once more. Deep red, irritated sores covered her right hand. They travelled up her wrist. Small pockets of yellow pus oozed from the worst ones along her fingers. I watched as she tucked a handkerchief around it, covering the sores from sight. A troubled look fell upon her features. *Is this what bird flu looks like?*

We moved down the aisles in silence. The rows of half empty shelves growing repetitive. They all looked generally the same with their sad contents and sagging metal. Everything in here seemed like remnants of an ancient and forgotten world.

"Stay right here I'm going to grab some pasta from the corner of the aisle," Mom said as she walked, her eyes lingering on me until she was out of sight. I waited, staring at the dull cans of corn in front of me. A small sigh escaped my lips. I noticed a flash of purple at the corner of my eye. I turned to look.

Ms. Vera stood at the end of the aisle, a can of green beans in her hand. Her shopping cart was full of different vegetables and fruits. She placed the green beans back on the shelf, a slightly perturbed look on her face. A can of whipped cream sat against a box of strawberries, clinking against the metal of the shopping cart as she pushed it. Her eyes met mine and her face lit up.

"Petra," She moved closer, coming around her cart to stand in front of me.

"Hi," I responded. Her smile was warm and inviting. Her satin purple blouse complete with a bow tied at the front. Her hair was curled and left to sit around her shoulders. She wore makeup, her face glowing with warmth against the white lights overhead. I smiled back.

"Is your dad here with you?" Her eyes searched the aisle.

"Nope, just Mom and I," I replied. Her smile dropped, her face turning pale. I turned to see Mom walking up from behind me, pasta in hand.

"Oh, sorry," Mom gave a sheepish smile. "I'm Petra's mom, you're her teacher, right? Ms…" Mom's voice trailed off as she tried to come up with her name.

"Vera," My teacher stuck her hand out. Mom waved her handkerchief covered hand.

"Sorry, had an accident at the work site," She looked embarrassed as she spoke, tucking her hand close to her body, trying to hide it from view. Mom picked at herself, pushing her hair behind her ears and trying to smooth her clothes. She looked uncomfortable.

"No, that's totally okay, I'm sorry I didn't notice," Ms. Vera said politely. Her body had gone rigid, her smile was no longer warm and inviting.

"How's Petra been at school?" Mom asked. I stepped away from them, staring down the aisle towards the shop windows. Their voices faded, muffled against my ears as I turned my attention elsewhere.

It looked darker outside. The trees that surrounded the courthouse shuffled with the breeze, their limbs bending and swaying aggressively back and forth. People held tightly to their cups and clothes as the wind tore at them with unparalleled ferocity. I felt my stomach churn, dread weaving its long, cold fingers around my body. A lump formed in my throat, static filling my ears. I watched as flocks of birds took to the air, flying quickly. They swarmed in droves, gliding through the wind, their wings flapping frantically.

Entire swarms collided with one another, feathers falling against the wind, squawks ringing out through the air as they moved, like alarms. The birds would dive and weave through each other, pushing to move faster and faster. Sweat beaded along my forehead, my heart beat quickened, and my knees trembled. My eyes followed their uneven patterns as my blood chilled; my ears rang. *They look like they're trying to escape.* The muffled voices surrounding me grew louder, closer, begging to be heard.

"Petra," I felt a hand on my shoulder, startling me. It was mom. She looked exhausted, much different to Ms. Vera who stood only a few feet away, arms crossed. "Are you okay?"

Mom watched me closely, her jaw tightening in that familiar way. Her eyes searched mine.

"Yeah, sorry it just looks windy outside," I pointed to the window. Both of their eyes followed the path of my finger, both nodding.

"I heard there's supposed to be a severe thunderstorm sometime this week," Ms. Vera sounded cold.

"Ah, then I guess we should get back home," Mom placed the pasta in the basket in her hand. "It was really nice to meet you sweetheart. Petra talks about you all the time. We should get together some day."

"Yeah," Ms. Vera's voice sounded soft, almost like it caught in her throat. She stole a quick glance at me, a small smile twitching at the corner of her mouth. She looked miserable.

"Bye," I waved.

"Goodbye Petra," She waved back.

We barely made it to the house in time. Mom's health was deteriorating fast. Her eyes looked heavy, the veins and whites of her eyes a thick dark red. Her face was flush giving her cheeks a deep rosy color. Her hair looked thin and her usual frizzy curls fell flat. Her breathing was slow and labored, her chest rising and falling in shallow breaths. Cough after cough wracked her body, her lungs hacked up thick mucus that she would spit to the ground.

Once inside she didn't bother with the groceries, dropping them to the floor and crawling up the stairs on all fours. The handkerchief had fallen around her hand, no longer able to hide the bleeding sores that had travelled further up her arm. The sores were a dark red, the skin puffed and pulled at the edges. Yellow pus collected in their centers. They looked angry and gross.

I looked at the groceries on the ground as the muffled coughs could be heard above me. The ceiling creaked and groaned against Mom's weight.

Grabbing the groceries I began to take them to the kitchen, until I heard it. A disgusting retching sound from above. I placed the milk on the counter, the sides filled with condensation. The retching began again. My hand slipped, the milk tumbling from my grasp. Time slowed as it fell, rolling from the counter and hitting the ground, the plastic rippling as it connected with the floor.

Milk spilled along the tiles, coating my shoes and splashing against my legs. Panic filled my blood as I rushed to grab towels from the laundry room. I desperately tried to wipe away at the trail of footprints I left. The towels didn't seem to do much against the milk. Instead, it looked more like the towels were averse to soaking up the white liquid, preferring to just push it around and deeper into the grout of the tiles.

My hands moved quickly, my mind swirling. The sounds of gagging and heaving grew louder. I stood, stomping my feet against the towel, begging it to pick up the milk, but it refused. I took a second, staring at the mess, the broken plastic sitting still against the floor. *It'll have to wait.*

I ripped my shoes off and rushed upstairs. The lights weren't turned on. Shadows loomed against the walls, the wind howling against the window. Mom and Dad's bathroom door sat wide open. I slowed, craning my neck to peer inside from a distance. My hands shook.

Mom was slumped against the toilet, her eyes closed, barely breathing.

"Mom!" I sprinted to her, but even with me trying to lift her head she was limp. "Mom please." I felt tears pricking at the back of my eyes. My breath hitched when my eyes connected with the toilet. Thick black vomit pooled and splashed the sides with a deep crimson color. The stench was putrid, assaulting my nose and making me gag.

I poked and prodded, even shaking her, but she wouldn't move. Her eyelids remained closed as her lungs wheezed. *What do I do? What do I do?*

My eyes searched frantically for anything that could be of use. The bathroom was mostly empty. I tried once more to pick up her head, but as I did a clump of her hair detached itself from her scalp, tangling in my fingers. I shook my hand, trying to get them off, watching as they floated through the air to the ground.

Her phone. It sat in her pocket, the outline sharp against the sweats. I grabbed at it, turning it on and swiping at it to open. I dialed as quickly as my fingers could.

It rang once…twice…three times…then it cut off.

"What?" My voice broke. I tried it again. It rang once, then sent to voicemail. I tried again and again and again.

"Hello?" *Finally!*

"Dad!" My voice was shrill. "Please-"

"Petra? What're you doing on your mom's phone?" He sounded annoyed. There was a faint sound behind him, a voice, then the clinking of glasses and sounds of music.

"Mom is sick," I said quickly. Confusion pulled at me but I pushed it aside.

"Yeah, I know, she'll be fine-"

"No, Mom is really sick," I tried to fill my voice with as much urgency as I could, but it didn't take.

"What do you want me to do?" He let out a sigh. "I can't just up and leave work, I'm busy."

"But she won't wake up and she keeps throwing up," The tears now fell along my cheeks, surprising me. Silence. Static crackled against my ear as I waited. *What do I do*?

"Okay," His voice was quiet. "Call an ambulance."

The line went dead.

I stared blankly at the phone for a second, my tears creating little droplets against the screen. My fingers felt numb as I dialed the three numbers.

"Hello 911 what's your emergency?" The operator's voice was warm but firm.

"I need an ambulance," My voice cracked against the words.

"Okay, what's the emergency?"

I curled up against Mom's side. She felt cold.

"My mom won't wake up and she's sick," I sniffed, snot running from my nose. Then I felt it, like something inside me snapped.

I sobbed uncontrollably. Panicked, loud, heaving cries fell from my throat. The operator was nice, trying to comfort and calm me down, but I couldn't.

This can't be real. I sat on the edge of the porch wrapped in a thin white blanket, though the wind had died down. A paramedic sat next to me. His name was Brad.

The flashing of the red and blue lights was bright against the grey of the surrounding world. A group of people were currently getting the stretcher into the back of the ambulance, a long IV had been placed in Mom's arm already. She looked like the mummies she so carefully digs up. Her skin was tight and shiny, her hair thin and frail. *This can't be real.*

"Do you want to ride in the back of the ambulance or with a cop?" Brad's voice was higher than expected. The kind of high nasally voice most people complain about.

"Can I ride with my mom?" My voice was broken. My entire body felt numb.

"Yeah, of course kiddo," Brad stood. The ruffling of his clothes loud. I winced. I followed close to him, he kept his hand against my back between my shoulder blades, guiding me forward. I climbed into the back, the other paramedics trying their best to give me small reassuring smiles.

"You're dad's a doctor, yeah?" Brad asked as he closed the doors.

"Yeah," I nodded, my eyes staring at my mom. She looked lifeless. Tears coated my eyes again. I turned away. My eyes met with a young woman. She had dirty blonde hair pulled into a slick bun. She smiled, shiny braces sat along her teeth. My eyes fell to my hands. Brad patted me on the shoulder.

The ride to the hospital was quiet and rough. The ambulance didn't seem to have much for suspension. Every bump or pothole that caught the wheels felt like the whole thing might tip over and roll.

The worst part was the siren. It was ungodly loud. Its high-pitched shrieks pierced my ears. I was left with a headache by the time we reached the hospital. A short, ten-minute ride where I got to watch Mom's body flailing against the harsh suspension.

Once at the hospital, everyone piled out of the ambulance in a hurry. They rushed Mom inside and me with her.

The hospital smelled sterile and clean. The walls and ceiling were white. I felt uncomfortable as we pushed down the halls, slamming doors open. I was almost running to keep up, Brad making sure I stayed with the group. People watched us as we passed, their heads turning at the frantic noise.

Then it was quiet. We were placed in a small room with no roommate. The nurses had run to Mom's side poking at her and checking her vitals. Brad had me stand with him a few feet away while we waited.

They swarmed her like ants. Crawling around her body. They talked in codes, moving quickly as they shuffled papers back and forth. A clipboard was passed around and then placed at the end of the hospital bed. Mom hadn't stirred once since I found her.

"Everything's going to be alright, kiddo," Brad patted my shoulder again. I looped my finger through his belt loop. He ruffled my hair, leaving his hand on my head. "I promise."

I felt nothing, as if my body wasn't my own. I was watching a movie play out while I stared down at myself. My mind was silent and eventually the sounds of shuffling and words began to drown out and fade to slight muted sounds. My eyes were heavy and sore from crying.

An hour passed. Doctors and nurses kept coming and leaving, not really saying much. My legs grew stiff standing and waiting. My eyes remained on Mom.

"Why don't you have a seat, kiddo?" Brad pulled up a chair. It was one of those weirdly angled plastic chairs. The kind that have metal legs and are cold all over. I shivered.

"I'm okay," I turned my attention back to Mom. Brad nodded, pulling the chair toward himself to sit. I kept my finger in his belt loop as he sat, just slightly to the side so my finger didn't get pinched against the side of the chair.

I was thankful for Brad. He seemed to be the only source of comfort I had in the cold of the hospital. The nurses wouldn't look at me and nothing the doctors said made any sense. I was confused, hungry, and upset, but

Brad was steady. He was like a strong tree that blocked the wind, or a rock in the center of a creek.

He didn't have to stay but he did, and that's what matters. He could've left me here by myself with Mom asleep, or he could've left me with the cops at the station. But Brad was a good person. He had a daughter of his own. I'd imagine he would hope someone would stay with her too in this situation.

"Hey," A familiar voice. My head snapped to its direction. Dad stood in the hall, running a hand through his hair as he spoke to a nurse and adjusted his white coat. He nodded a few more times before coming into the room, stealing a quick glance at me. I let go of Brad's belt loop. A waft of a sickly-sweet scent followed Dad into the room. I scrunched my nose.

Brad stood, stretching his legs. "Dr. Craven, you're the kiddo's father, yeah?"

Dad took a second to look him up and down before stretching out his hand to shake. "Yeah, I'm Petra's father."

Brad shook his hand with the faintest hesitation. His eyes flitted to me and back to Dad an odd look scrawled along his features.

"I need to get to work," Dad turned away and began to examine Mom. Brad stood for a moment, staring at my parents.

"Well, he seems like loads of fun," Brad mumbled under his breath. His eyes lingered on my parents for a few more seconds before turning to me as he crouched down.

"Kiddo, if you need anything just call the nonemergency line, okay?"

"The nonemergency line?" I asked. He nodded.

"Yeah, you call that number and ask for me and I'll swing by to keep you safe," He gave a small smile, his mustache bunching up at the corners. "If not me, then one of my buddies you met earlier. Either way, you'll be safe."

I nodded. "Okay."

"Bye Dr. Craven," Brad stood waving toward Dad, but Dad didn't even acknowledge him.

Another hour passed, but this time I stood next to an empty cold chair, in a mostly empty cold room. Dad met with several of the nurses and other doctors, discussing things and going over different paperwork each time. New tests and new paperwork seemed to come through every few minutes.

My body ached. My hips and knees pleaded with me to sit, but I refused. Everything hurt all at once and yet I was cold. I was cold down to the very marrow of my bones. The unwelcoming crisp air enveloped me in a wintry blanket, sinking deep into my skin.

"Alright," Dad stood in front of me, blocking my view of Mom. "You ready to go home?"

His face looked calm, almost completely unconcerned. His voice felt as cold as the room.

"What about Mom?" I asked, trying to peer around his legs to see her. From the space between his legs, I could see her hand twitch and lift. A nurse moved to her bedside.

"She's fine, she's just got a little cold," Dad sighed. He looked annoyed as he ran his fingers through his hair.

"A cold?" I could feel my face contort in disbelief. I'd had colds before, and never once had I looked the way Mom did. I'd drink chicken noodle soup and maybe cough a little bit, but Mom looked like she was holding hands with Death himself. "But-"

"She's just a little dehydrated and has a fever," He dismissed me with the rolling of his eyes.

"What about her hand," I pointed to my right hand where the sores would be along Mom's.

"She likely got into some poison ivy or something while digging around in that shi-sorry-site at home," He was quick to come up with answers, but it wasn't sitting right with me. Something felt off.

"Dad," I whined.

"Petra, look she's fine," The annoyance was much clearer in his voice as he glared at me. "She's going to take some cold medicine and put ointment on her arm, alright? Everything is fine, we're going home."

So that's it? He moved away from me, walking toward the hallway.

"Did you pick food up for Mom and I?" He stopped at my question. He turned to look at me, blinking a few times.

"What're you talking about?" He looked puzzled.

"You were out eating dinner, right? I could hear it in the background of the phone call," Mom turned to look at us, her smile dropping as she listened.

Dad hesitated, his brow furrowing. "I wasn't at dinner. I was here for my shift." The nurse by the door gave him a sharp look. "I don't know what you think you heard, but I was here. If you're hungry, we can make something at home."

He walked away, his cheeks burning red, to speak with a few of the other doctors. The nurse at the door glanced at me before following. I turned back to Mom.

She looked better now. She was alert and talking with the nurses. *Maybe it is just a cold*. Afterall, Dad is a doctor, right?

Mom turned to me with a reassuring smile adorning her lips. Her teeth were yellow and her gums bleeding. I gave a small smile back. My stomach filled with dread.

That's not a cold.

<u>Six</u>

The familiar sound of stifled voices drifted through the gap under my door. I neared the it, once again opening it just enough. Both of my parents stood in the hallway, speaking in hushed stage whispers.

"Stop, just stop," Dad raised his hand, his eyes angry. Mom looked upset. She wore a similar outfit to the one from earlier in the day, except her sweats and shirt were both black. Mom looked frail and desperate. Her hair was even thinner than before and the bags under her eyes were darker as if her eyes were sinking further into her skull. Her skin was pale against the dark clothes.

"Can we please not do this tonight?" Dad asked.

"Do what?" Mom gave him an odd look.

"You're trying to start a fight and I'm not in the mood to deal with you right now," Dad sighed.

"But," Her voice was soft. "Petra said she heard-"

"I don't give a fuck what she thinks she heard," He spat. "You want to believe her over me? A child who was panicking over you having a cold? Really?" He looked at her incredulously.

"I passed out," Mom's voice was uncharacteristically angry. "What did you want her to do? Leave me there until you decided to come home?"

"I told you I had a shift at the hospital and would be home late," He retorted. "Again, it's not my fault you can't remember these things." He began to walk toward the spare room.

"We both know our daughter doesn't lie," She crossed her arms. "Who were you out with?"

Dad whipped around to face her. "Who do you think? No really tell me. Who the fuck would I be out with?"

"I don't-"

"Exactly," He flung his arms out aggressively. "I bust my ass to take care of you two and this is what you think of me? I fund your little dirt hobby, and you sit here and accuse *me*?"

"I would never-"

"You actively are," Dad cut her off again. Mom coughed a few times, wiping away at her eyes. "Do you really think so little of me? Did I not help you at the hospital?"

There was a pause.

"I'm just scared," Her voice was barely audible. "I've never felt this sick before. My hair is falling out, look at my arm, I-" Her voice cracked as she fell to her knees, sobbing. Dad's shoulders tensed.

"Get up Terra, for fucks sake," His voice was cold. "Stop acting like a child."

Mom continued to cry on the floor, hugging her arms around her body. Dad blew out a breath. She looked up at him as she spoke.

"What happened to us?"

Dad didn't respond. Instead, he stared down at her, his face stoic. His eyes looked cruel as he watched her. His hands clenched at his sides. He looked up at the ceiling, relaxing his hands and shoulders, before looking down at her again.

"I'm going to bed, when you're done with your little tantrum take your medicine."

And with that he disappeared into the spare room. Mom stayed crumpled on the floor. Her small frame was semi-hidden in the shadows of the hall. A few minutes passed until she stood, closing the bedroom door behind her.

Sleep didn't come easy. My eyes were heavy and my body was tired, but I couldn't. Every time I tried to sleep my mind would race, static would fill my ears, and my eyes would snap to the gap under my door, searching for those shadowed feet.

Instead, I took to reading. Mom had bought me several books on dinosaurs and extinct animals. The pages were filled with depictions of fossils and descriptions of where they used to reside.

I didn't bother to actually read any of the descriptions. Sleep kept tugging at my eyes and if I did decide to read my head would hit the pillow. Instead, my eyes skimmed the pages, hovering over the words and images for a few seconds. The pages were thick and murmured against the friction between my fingers My head nodded, my body filling with cement. Everything felt heavy and my bed was warm and soft. I made eye contact with my dinosaur plush off to my right.

I turned to face the door. It had been silent for a long time. The moon had long since reached its peak as it hung in the sky illuminating the sheep in the fence. I hadn't seen the feet under the gap, nor had I heard the obnoxious scratching I did the previous night. Everything was completely still, as if the house itself were sleeping.

A twinge of hunger hit my stomach. I stared at the gap under the door for a bit longer, waiting. My mouth grew dry and my throat felt like I swallowed sand.

Nothing is going to happen. Even as I thought the words I couldn't believe them. I felt frozen. Stuck in place in my bed where it was safe. But the growling of my stomach grew less and less possible to ignore.

My feet touched the cold of the hardwood as I left my small space of safety. The floorboards creaked and groaned against my weight, whispering to everyone in the house that I was still awake. The gap under my door remained empty. Unease crept over me like a cold and unwanted blanket. My stomach knotted and turned as I neared the door.

I leaned an ear against it, listening. But there was only silence to greet my ears. I let out the breath I had been holding. *Maybe it was all just a bad dream.*

The door creaked open slowly against its rusty hinges. My hair stood at the noise, my pulse quickened and my skin chilled. But once it was open there was nothing. Only darkness greeted me. The shadows of the hallway stood still and the boxes along the wall still held the same dust as before. I let out a breath of relief.

The stairs made little noise against my socks. The house was completely still and quiet. Any noises that did make their way through the night carried through the walls softly. I reached the kitchen, grabbed the step stool and a glass.

The kitchen sink overlooked the tree Mom and I had buried the bird under. The smooth metal of the faucet gleamed in the moonlight. It was cold against my hands as I turned the water on, the sound loud in the stillness of the house. Then I heard it.

The very sound chilled my blood, my eyes widened. My reflection stared back at me with fear riddled features. I turned to face the dining table. The gold metal shinned bright against the dark wood. The lion's head held still as the legs performed their slow, ritualistic dance. My stomach churned and my heart beat against my chest. The legs *tick*, *tick*, *ticked*, until they stopped. A goat's leg hanging over the lion this time, its empty eyes watching, waiting.

The glass slipped from my hand in a loud crash, the water splashing across the counter and floor. I scrambled off the step stool, falling to the floor as my feet tripped. My knee hit the ground first, my hands catching most of my weight as I was pitted forward.

I held my breath, staring at the stairs, waiting for the inevitable rush of feet as my parents scrambled down the stairs.

But they didn't. There was no flurry of motion, no sounds of footsteps along the floorboards, just complete silence. I felt my blood run cold.

A hand trailed along the very edge of the stairs I could see before disappearing into the darkness above. I blinked a few times trying to make sense of it. *They didn't check on me?*

Maybe they heard me fall but saw me on the ground and thought I'd be okay? Maybe they saw me lift my head? Or maybe they didn't see me at all?

I pushed myself up, my knee aching as I put weight on it. A bruise had already begun to form against my knee cap. My hands were shaking. I moved for the stairs, caution fueling my movement as I tried to walk as quietly as possible. The floorboards remained hushed as I walked, holding their breath, helping me hide.

I was halfway up the stairs when I heard it. *Thump. Thump. Thump.* I paused. My blood felt like ice, my heart trying to break free of my chest, and my ears filled with static. I closed my eyes. I tried to focus on my breathing, but my lungs were shaking. My next steps were uncertain and unbalanced.

As I reached the top of the stairs my eyes widened. Mom stood at the wall by her bedroom door. Her hair was tangled and matted. Her clothes were torn, hanging in tatters against her thin frame. Her bones seemed to push against her skin, as if her flesh had been vacuum sealed on. Her head hit the wall. *Thump. Thump. Thump.*

My jaw trembled, tears collecting in my eyes, my mind drawing blank. I could feel fear winding its way around my body, digging its nails into the depths of my soul. She continued to hit her head against the wall in quick succession, never pausing.

I continued up the stairs, reaching the landing and staying crouched. I wouldn't turn my back to her, instead, I moved slowly, keeping my body low, avoiding soft spots in the floor I knew would make noise. The carpet muffled my steps.

As I neared the halfway point I felt my heart jump to my throat. She slammed her head into the wall harder, faster. *Thump. Thump. Thump.*

I held my breath, knowing that if I tried to breathe the sound would give me away. I watched in terror as the wall started to stain red. Her movements were jerky and odd, her arms straight at her sides, flailing in a rigid swaying motion. Her body was completely rigid.

I began to move again, drawing closer to my door. The sound of her head hitting the wall growing faster and faster. I felt tears falling from my eyes, trailing down my face. I turned to see how close I was to the door.

Only a few feet. I could make it. I could climb into bed and forget this ever happened. I –

The floorboard groaned under my weight, the sound sharp against my ears. My body froze. Mom stopped. I didn't dare to move. My heart raced, my jaw clenched, tears blurred my vision. I blinked at them, trying to keep my eyes on her.

Her head snapped to me. My heart dropped to my stomach. A disgusting gurgled scream tore from her throat. She rushed me, inhumanely fast. Her arms outstretched, her fingers gnarled and twisted. Her face felt wrong, her brow bone too far forward, her eyes dark and sunken in, and her teeth sharp and pointed.

I screamed, sprinting to my door. I could hear her behind me. The primal howl and deep wheezing of her lungs so close. I could almost feel her fingers in my hair or against my shirt. My entire body felt like it was on fire as I ran. The static in my ears grew louder, my mind grew fuzzy, and my vision grew dark around the edges.

I dove across the threshold of my door, slamming it and holding my feet against it to keep it closed. The door shook as Mom slammed against it. The sound of her nails scratching at the wood made my hair stand up. My lungs burned, my breathing ragged. She screamed those ugly, wet screams.

My eyes landed on the small dresser against the wall to my right. I reached for it, stretching my body as far as it could, my legs bracing against Mom's tirade. My fingers just barely skimmed the surface of the bottom of the dresser. I let out the breath I had been holding.

Please. I tried again, my left foot now only keeping my toes on the door. The door jolted against its hinges, desperately holding her back.

My fingers connected this time, gripping the underside of the dresser. It scooted along the floor slowly. I grunted with the effort. Tears now streamed down my face, the door slamming. I continued pulling, getting more fingers on it, pulling harder.

Please.

The dresser crawled along the floor, as if it didn't want to get anywhere near the door. As if it too were afraid. But I willed it. I pulled as hard as I could, getting it closer to the door before it finally toppled over. Clothes and trinkets spilled from the drawers as I moved out of the way. It crashed to the ground, some of the wood splintering and snapping against the weight. I pushed it up against the door as far as it would go. But it wasn't enough.

Each slam of the door pushed it further and further in. The hinges squealed in agony as they fought to hold it in place. The dresser lurched forward with each bang. My breathing was too fast. My hands were too shaky. But I couldn't stop.

I grabbed my bed. The only other heavy thing in the room. Pushing it across the floor. It tore against the hardwood, leaving large trails etched into the wood.

Please stop.

Mom continued. Scratching and howling. Her body slammed into the door. I could see her through the gap she had created. Her smile was wide and unsettling and her eyes wild. She slammed into the door again and again.

I pushed the legs of the bed around the dresser so the bed would fit over it. My muscles screamed, my pulse in my throat and ears. I could barely see. My ears filled with static my eyesight growing dark. The bed lurched against the door causing me to fall back. I got up, pushing the bed forward. With each slam of the door the bed would push against me.

Please.

My entire body screamed, the very fibers of my muscles snapping and breaking. My mind was on fire, burning white hot, searing panic against my soul. I wanted to throw up but I couldn't. I had to survive.

With a final push the bed was against the door. I fell back. Time slowed. The world spun, tilting in a spiraling wash of colors. The noise grew dull, the static quieting. I felt dizzy and exhausted. The scratching continued, slowly fading out. I felt like I was floating. My body being carried on the waves of the sea. The world moved and undulated in slow motion. The colors of my room mixed with the shapes and shadows of the night.

My head hit the floor. My body was on fire, burning and painful. My lungs stopped, my chest no longer rising. Everything was still. Everything was silent.

<u>Seven</u>

"Petra!"

I blinked a few times. The world came into view. My ceiling fan turned in lazy circles. My entire body ached.

"Petra! Petra!" The door handle to my room jiggled. I lifted my head to watch. The door not budging against the barricade I had created last night. "Petra open the door!"

It was Dad. I could recognize his voice, but my body felt too weak to move. I didn't want to. I just wanted to lay there against the cold hardwood and sleep. I wanted to drift away. To forget everything that's happened and rest.

"Petra please!" I sighed at his words, closing my eyes. "Petra open the fucking door!" Though he cursed he didn't sound angry. Instead, he sounded…scared. Something I'd never heard from his voice before. It shook his words and formed a lump in his throat. His voice sounded hoarse.

There was a crack, the door opening ever so slightly as everything pushed away. I sat up.

"Petra!" He screamed. Footsteps, then another slam as things moved. His hand came through the gap, pushing at the headboard of the bed. The door opened just enough for him to squeeze through. "Petra, oh my god."

He rushed to my side, hugging me close. I didn't react. I couldn't. I just sat there.

"You're freezing," Dad said as he rubbed my arms. I leaned my head against his chest, closing my eyes.

"I'm tired," The words barely croaked out of me, broken and frail.

"I know," He held me closer. "Me too."

My forehead sat on the wood table. I stared down at my hands. My eyes trailed along the ridges and intricate lines of my palms. My entire body felt disconnected.

"Good morning," I sat up. Mom smiled, her yellowed teeth and blackened, bleeding gums on full display. I cringed. "Does anybody want breakfast?"

Dad and I shared a scared glance. He shook his head.

"No, I'm good, I'm about to head to work," He pulled at the collar of his white coat. His skin was almost the same color. Dark circles lined his eyes, and his hair looked greasy. Mom's smile faded.

"You never want to stay for breakfast," She threw the pan back into the cabinet. The noise jarring against the otherwise calm of the house. She let out a breath. Dad stood stone still. "Sorry, I don't know what came over me for a second there."

Mom laughed, but not her usual laugh. It felt different. Higher in pitch and shorter. Her laugh usually shook her whole body and would often be accompanied by a snort. This laugh was short, small and almost giggly.

"Okay, well I'll be going now," Dad's eyes flicked to mine. He hesitated. His eyes lingered on me for a moment. "Let me know if you need anything."

I watched as he left. He didn't turn to look back when he opened the door. No, instead, he chose to face forward, away from me.

My eyes moved across the house, trailing over the medallion once more, the lion's vacant eyes all too familiar now. My gaze continued their path landing on Mom. She didn't look like herself. Her skin looked like paper mâché stretched across a skeleton of thin bones. Her eyes were sunken in, her cheek bones pronounced, and her hair was nearly all gone. Little tufts and strands still held desperately to her head, refusing to let go. Large blue veins latticed her body in a weaving pattern. She wore her usual outfit of button-down shirt and jeans, but the clothes were baggy and weren't ironed.

Just yesterday she looked on the verge of death and even now she still did but for some reason she was acting just shy of normal. She was chipper and happy, humming and singing as she twirled what strands of hair she had left along her finger.

She turned to me. That unsettling smile still glued to her face. I swallowed. "Do you want to come feed the sheep with me?"

"Okay," My voice was weak, tired.

"Alright let's go," She skipped to the door. I had never seen her skip before. It looked oddly child-like and uncoordinated.

I followed her outside, keeping a bit of distance between us. The world outside looked even worse than she did. The ground looked more like sand. There was no moisture left in it to be dirt anymore. The trees stood in twisted patches, their limbs completely bare. The grass was yellow and broken, small fragments of them snapping away against the wind.

My breath hitched as I turned to the sheep. They stood, motionless. Not a single one of them made a noise or movement. They didn't flick their ears or their tails. They didn't chew or reach their heads down for grass. Instead, they stared at Mom. As she drew near the sheep moved away, never taking their eyes off her. They avoided her like a wave, backing away in eerie silence.

"Good morning my little sheep," Mom grinned from ear to hear, bending down to get closer, but they refused. "Come here, everything is okay." She reached out her hands, but they wouldn't draw near. Her smile didn't fade. She didn't even look upset. She just stood and dusted her hands, continuing to hum a melody I hadn't heard before.

I followed her into the barn where I watched her rip open a bag of feed and dump it on the ground.

"What're you doing?" I asked. Her eyes snapped to mine.

"What? I'm feeding them silly," She spread the feed out with her hands, throwing it closer to the sheep who stayed a few feet away.

"We never feed them like that," I said, watching as the pellets would hit them in the head and stick in their fur. But they didn't so much as blink.

"What?" Mom stopped.

"We put the food in the trough," I pointed a finger at the black box sitting in the center of the fenced area. Her smile dropped.

"Well, I didn't want to do it like that today," She grabbed more feed in her hands chucking it at me. I put my hands up to deflect some of the pieces. "God forbid I wanted to do something *different*."

Her eyes seethed with rage, today was full of firsts.

"Okay," I responded, trying to deescalate the situation. "Then we can do it like this."

She stopped throwing the feed at me, her creepy smile returned. It stretched and pulled at her lips in an odd angle. She started to hum again. It was an oddly paced melody. It seemed like the tune was too fast for its drawn-out notes.

"Why don't we go dig a little bit?" Mom asked. She was still, watching the sheep as they watched her.

"Sure," I could feel the lump forming in my throat as the hair on the back of my neck stood up.

"Let's get going then," Her smile grew wider, the blackened scabs along her gums tearing and bleeding further. I reeled back a bit.

Mom didn't hold the same brisk pace as before that had me jogging to keep up. Instead, she walked through the brush with ease, barely moving the branches and twigs aside. The branches would catch at her remaining strands of hair, tugging and pulling them from her scalp. They would tear at her skin, creating delicate lines of white in their wake. She didn't once look back to make sure I was keeping up.

Coming to the clearing it looked nearly identical as before. The only difference was the decay. The entire forest surrounding it was falling apart. The limbs of the trees were broken and jagged, laying against each other in odd angles. There was no grass left, just withered sticks and empty dirt that was dry and cracked. Shriveled and brittle leaves decorated the ground in deep browns.

Mom got into the hole that we had dug into Friday. She looked excited, her body operating quickly in awkward jolting movements. Her hands dug at the earth, nails tearing into the cracked dirt in a feverish frenzy. More bones and flowers were unearthed as she dug.

"Hand me some of those containers," She waved a hand at me. "Quickly."

I grabbed as many of the clear plastic boxes as I could, fumbling with the lids in my hands as I slid into the hole with her. She tore them from my arms, tossing them to the side. She laid out three containers. In one she'd place the small bones, the second was the flowers, and the third was the sealed papers. She was careful with each one, studying and caressing the artifacts as she hummed sweetly to them. It made me uncomfortable.

I wrung my hands and bit my lip, trying to calm my restless nerves. The wind picked up through the trees, rustling their branches and leaves.

"Here, take these back to the house," Mom shoved two of the three containers into my arms, still piling more in the third.

I set the boxes on the edge of the dig site, climbing up. The dirt fell around my wrists as my knee tried to hold my weight against the edge. But the dirt fell away faster than I could react, one of the boxes tumbling, rolling through the air and crashing to the ground. There was an enraged scream to my right. My body was snatched back, a hard grip shooting pain through my shoulders.

"What is wrong with you?" Mom's voice was loud and irate. Her pupils were pin pricks, her face mad. Shock froze me in place as she gripped tighter, her fingers digging into my skin.

"I'm sorry," I choked against the words. Panic and fear wrapped around my chest and lungs.

"You little bitch," She shoved me away from her. I stumbled, barely catching myself. "How are you so useless?"

As she stepped forward, I retreated instinctively. I cowered in on myself, tears flooding my eyes. My heart was beating too fast, my pulse too loud.

"Get the fuck out of here," She kicked the dirt at me, the cloud of dust obscuring her from view. "If you so much as breathe on those boxes wrong I'll beat you within an inch of your life, do you understand?"

I nodded, quickly picking up the box and placing it further from the edge this time. My entire body shook as I scrambled out of there, my pace fast, my mind racing. I'd never heard Mom yell before. She's never once threatened me. I could feel the tears running down my cheeks as terror forced me to stop. My muscles constricted.

I couldn't breathe. I doubled over, making sure to set the boxes down gently. I fell to my hands and knees, my vision growing dark and static once against filled my ears. My body convulsed, my shoulders burning where she had touched. My fingers dug into the ground, desperately trying to find anything to hold onto. The world was spinning around me, the forest a blur of color and motion. I coughed. The sound shook my lungs and pierced my throat. I coughed again. The feeling of burning hot liquid filling my throat and lungs. *I can't breathe.*

I began to crawl through the underbrush. My hands swiped away at leaves and twigs, splinters driving deep into the palms of my hands, but I couldn't stop. I needed to get away. Then came another round of coughs, attacking my body from the inside. I choked, grabbing my throat and suddenly I vomited.

The burning sensation that had filled my lungs disappeared, my vision and hearing returned.

I took a moment. Staring down at the congealed and black mess beneath me I felt utter disbelief. Snot fell from my nose as tears continued to fall.

What is happening?

I felt the hair prick along the back of my neck, my skin growing cold. My gaze drifted along the trees and grass.

There was nothing. No wind to rustle the branches, no squirrels and birds to play among the trees, no insects crawling between the debris. It was completely, unnervingly, disgustingly quiet.

My entire body froze in fear as my gaze continued to travel along the trees and then my heart stopped. My eyes were met with an unholy sight.

The sheep stared at me. They lined the fence. Their large eyes vacant and waiting. They didn't twitch, or flick their tails or bend their heads, no, they stood perfectly still, waiting.

I swallowed, wiping at my nose and mouth and slowly standing up. My body trembled. I grabbed the boxes and began walking to the house. My eyes remained on the sheep, but theirs remained facing where I'd come from. They didn't even seem to notice me. I stopped for a second to watch them, to take in just how still they were. A fly landed on the eye of one, but they didn't blink. I felt my heart beating in my chest, the static growing in my ears again. I followed their gaze into the forest. My stomach churned as every fiber of my being screamed to run.

They're staring at Mom.

<u>Eight</u>

It was the same song and dance every night. It never changed. Dinner, just me and Mom, Dad comes home late, they argue, and everyone sleeps.

Until recently. I don't think I've slept nearly enough the last two nights, nor did I feel like I was going to be able to sleep tonight. Though my eyes grew heavy and my mind would drift, my body was jolted awake. It would rip me away from that peaceful slumber I so desperately needed.

I sat by the door, waiting for the same song and dance that has occurred every night for the last few months. It was the only thing that hadn't changed.

Dad stood outside their bedroom door. His shoulders were tense as if he were bracing for the fight. His lips were pursed and his hands were clenched.

But none came. Mom stepped out of the bathroom, humming that same awful tune from earlier today. She wore her robe tied tightly around her thinning frame. Her skin looked like paper, like it could be ripped off by the slightest breeze. What remained of her hair was soaked. Small water droplets glistened in the moonlight and fell to the floor. She didn't look at Dad, instead walking straight to their room.

"Where are you going?" Dad's voice was hushed and confused. He reached out a tentative hand.

"To bed," Mom stopped in the doorway. She turned to face him, a smile set against her lips.

"You don't want to ask me where I've been?" Dad's brow furrowed. "You don't want to accuse me of anything?"

"Guilty conscience?" Mom tilted her head to the left.

"What?" Dad stepped back.

"If you're not doing anything wrong, I don't have anything to accuse you of, right?" Mom stepped toward him. "Unless you did something wrong and want me to punish you."

"No, I didn't-"

"Good," Mom turned to head back into the room, the door shutting loudly.

Dad stood there, mouth agape. He looked…lost. His shoulders dropped and his hands released. A few minutes went by before he hesitantly moved to the spare room. His steps were uncertain as he did. Before closing the spare room door, he took another lingering look at the door Mom had shut so willingly.

I closed my own door. The soft thud echoing that of my parents. It felt wrong. *Why?*

Have I become so used to Mom and Dad's constant bickering and nightly arguments that the one night they don't it makes me uncomfortable? Or was it the way Mom handled it? Completely calm and almost happy?

I sighed at the thoughts, climbing into bed and laying down. The covers were soft and warm. The smell of the lavender laundry detergent spilling through the air as I brought the comforter under my chin. My stuffed animals created a small divet in the mattress with their weight. I could feel myself being lulled to sleep, my eyes watching the door. I tried to fight it, terrified of what might happen if I were to let myself drift, but I couldn't. As soon as my eyes shut I was asleep.

I awoke, groggy, with a headache. My eyes struggled to stay open. Everything felt hot as my ears started to pick it up. The static was back. It was loud and grating against the silence of the house, but there was something else. It lay in the background just faint enough that it would slip away. I focused on the sound, trying to push through the static.

Whispers. My eyes snapped open as I sat up. Overlapping voices chanted in heavy whispers just behind the static. I couldn't understand the foreign language, but the chant continued. It chanted along at the same rhythm as my heart. My pulse quickened, fear coiling tightly around my throat. I put my hands over my ears, but they couldn't be silenced. They grew louder, the static fading into the cacophony of voices. My eyes met with the door and my heart sank.

It's open. The whispers and static stopped. The sounds of scraping echoed through the hall, like claws digging into hardened dirt. I stood on trembling legs, making my way to the hall as quietly as I could.

Peering over the doorframe I didn't see anything out of the ordinary. Mom's door was open, but other than that there was nothing.

There was only the moonlight stretching its long fingers across the shadows in the hall. The boxes held the same dust, the hall bare. I let out the breath I'd been holding. Then it came again, the scraping and scratching, but this time it sounded closer. My eyes trailed up, following the shadows along the ceiling, following the bumpy texture of the paint.

I froze. My heart slammed against my chest and my stomach dropped.

Mom?

She had somehow wedged her body into the corner of the ceiling close to the window on the far side. She faced outward as her hands and feet dug into the walls, pushing her shoulders and hips into the corner. Her eyes stared at the spare bedroom door, her teeth sharp.

I watched in horror as she moved, crawling along the wall like an inverted bug. Her movements were uncanny and unnatural. Her fingers would dig into the drywall before she would extend her foot. Her nails chipped the paint, scarring the walls as little bits of white powder fell to the floor.

She reached the spare bedroom door, turning her arms the right way as she climbed headfirst toward the handle. She opened it with ease as she sat upside down clinging to the door frame with her fingers and feet. Then she went in, pulling herself back to the ceiling with the door frame and disappearing into the darkness.

That's not my mother. Everything in me was screaming to run. Every fiber of my muscles, every cell in my body, and every hair on my head was begging me to escape.

But I held my breath instead. It was so quiet. The silence was excruciating. My lungs burned.

I jumped as a sudden loud and guttural screech echoed through the house. My heart raced and my head swam. I stepped out of the safety of my room. The screams continued. Primal and horrific shrieks of pain and confusion came from the spare bedroom. I swallowed as I moved down the hallway, taking small hesitant steps.

Suddenly, Dad burst from the room, panting. He scrambled to his feet, slamming the door just as Mom reached it. His muscles strained as he held it closed. His eyes searched the hall, desperate for anything that could help, until they landed on me.

"Petra?" I'd never seen this look in his eyes, nor had I heard his voice crack the way it did. He looked broken, terrified. It looked like dirt covered parts of his grey shirt and his arms were covered in blood and scratches. The skin looked red and raised. A slam rocked the door, tearing at the hinges, but Dad held steadfast. "Get me a rope or a bunch of belts, hurry."

I stared at him for a moment. His chest heaved and his muscles tightened against another hit. His jaw was clenched. *Is he crying*?

"Petra, hurry!" I stopped wasting time. I tore through the house, running down the stairs and out of the front door. My feet slammed against the cold dirt, small bits of broken grass and sharp sticks not breaking my stride. The sheep were still again. They stared at the second floor of the house this time. I ignored them, running for the barn.

Once inside I turned on the light. A warm yellow flicker bathed the room, before shutting off. The darkness was thick and suffocating. I tried the light switch again. Nothing.

Come on. Again, I flipped the switches, but there wasn't even a whisper of electricity. *Fine.*

I fumbled around in the dark, my hands clawing over everything they could. The wood along the walls was flaking, embedding little pieces of itself into my hands but I pressed on. My fingers fell over the cold metal of tools, the sharp teeth of saws, and the splintering wood of the cabinets and walls. *Please, it's got to be here.*

An inhuman shriek came from the direction of the house. Panic filled my lungs, static pushing into my ears.

I can find it. I moved my hands faster, my feet and shins bumping into tools and chairs along the ground. I winced in pain but refused to stop.

There! My hands felt the familiar feel of double braided rustic fibers. I pulled it from the table, the weight nearly taking me to the ground with it. I threw what I could over my shoulder, making a break for the house.

The screaming grew louder as I approached. It was becoming more feral and desperate. I could hear the pounding of the door from the bottom of the stairs. My heart raced and my stomach churned, dread and exhaustion weighing down my body. I lugged the rope over to Dad.

"Tie a knot around the doorknob," Dad said as I got closer. His feet were braced against the door frame as his hands gripped the handle, pulling the door closed. Another scream resounded from the room. I moved quickly, tying the end of the rope around the doorknob as tight as I could.

"Good, good job honey," Dad's voice was soft and encouraging. "Now go wrap it around the handle of Mom and I's room and pull as hard as you can. Do you understand?"

I nodded, grabbing the rope and sprinting to the other side of the hall. I did as he said, wrapping it around the handle and pulling. Dad started to let go of the door, but my strength wasn't enough. The door yanked free, a gap opening just enough to see the crazed eyes of Mom.

"Shit!" Dad grabbed the handle again, bracing himself against the door. "Give me the end you're holding."

I ran to him, he let go of the door with one and grabbing the rope with the other. He let go of the door, quickly grabbing the rope with both hands now and he pulled. He pulled with everything he had. Dad wrapped it around the spare bedroom handle before heading for their bedroom.

I watched in worry tainted awe as he struggled against the strength of Mom yanking the door. He tied it off around the handle of their shared bedroom, cranking the rope until it couldn't be any tighter. He checked the knot I had tied, tightening it a bit before backing away with caution.

We waited in silence, both held our breath as we watched. Mom pulled a few more times, but to no avail. The rope held and the door didn't budge. Dad let out a sigh of relief.

"Grab some clothes and your backpack, let's go," He pushed me toward my room. "We need to go so hurry."

Neither one of us spoke during the car ride. Dad kept to his usual habit of not turning on the radio, but this time I preferred it. I welcomed the silence.

When we pulled up to our destination, I was a bit confused. Dad was never much of a religious man. The church stared down at us in the gloom of the night and flickering streetlamps. It was an old building with large crosses decorating the front. Statues of angles sat at each side of the doors.

"Let's get inside," Dad pushed me forward and up the steps.

The doors groaned against their hinges as they swung open. The inside of the building smelled of fake roses and wet wood. The two rows of eight pews were perfectly aligned to face the front. A large cross with a statue depicting Jesus stood at the back wall. Three windows of stained glass representing different events in the Bible lined each of the side walls. It felt cold.

"Father," Dad rushed forward. A man stood in the center talking to a young woman but turned to look at us. He wore a long black robe with a small white piece on the collar. He was older than Dad, his hair peppered with bits of grey. He smiled, wrinkles lined his mouth and eyes.

"Hello, just a moment please," He held up his finger and turned back to the woman. He held her hand in his, not in the way Mom and Dad used to hold hands, but firm. They whispered a few solemn words back and forth. The woman's mascara had been running, creating large black smudges under her eyes.

She was a bit disheveled. Her hair was frizzy and dyed several colors, leaving it fried at the ends. Her clothes were a size too big, hanging off her small frame in an odd way. Her cheekbones were pronounced, and her nails were dirty. She had a busted lip and a bruise on her collarbone.

"Goodnight Maria," The priest kissed her forehead, and she left. "How can I help you, my son?"

Dad and I watched the woman for a second, the doors shutting with a loud and hallow echo.

"I need you to perform an exorcism," Dad spoke quickly. He looked rabid. His hands were shaking, his hair was a mess and eyes were wild. The priest gave him a sad look. I never knew Dad to be religious.

"Sir, I'm sorry but I don't do exorcisms," The priest shook his head.

"Then you know someone who does," Dad stepped closer, the priest looked worried.

"No," He shook his head. "Exorcisms aren't real, they were propaganda for the church, to exploit those with mental illness as poster children for demons we made up. We've done a lot of work trying to fix that image-"

"No, listen, I need a *real* exorcism," Dad interrupted. The priest's brow furrowed in confusion.

"There is nothing I can do for you, my son," He shrugged.

"Then call the Pope, or the Vatican," Dad was growing restless.

"You think I just have the Pope on speed dial?" The priest laughed incredulously.

"I-"

"Sir, I can assure you there is no such thing as demons. Man is the true monster in this world, not some vengeful spirit," The priest glanced at me before meeting Dad's eyes again. "Maybe you watch too many movies, eh?"

"You don't understand she's acting insane," Dad was fumbling his words, scrambling and rushed. "She's not making any sense, she doesn't even look like herself anymore, she's become angry and-"

"Anyone can be mean, sir, just because she's your wife doesn't mean she needs to tolerate-"

"She tried to kill me and our daughter," Dad interrupted again. The priest paused. His eyes flicked between both of us.

"Then that sounds like a job for the police," The priest shook his head as a sad look pulled at his features. "Or she needs to be institutionalized. Maybe both. But that's not for me to decide."

Dad ran a hand through his hair angrily. His face was turning a burning red, his eyes searching the walls and stained glass. The priest continued.

"You're more than welcome to stay the night here if you feel your daughter's life is in any danger," He gave me a wry smile. "Otherwise, I cannot help you. I'm sorry. May God forgive and protect you both."

"Yeah sure," Dad sounded defeated. His entire body deflated.

I learned the priest's name was Father Mallard, like the duck. He showed us the bathrooms and had a nun help me clean myself up with a wet rag. Meanwhile, Dad ordered us a pizza so we could eat since I'd complained I was hungry. He didn't eat any of it, sitting in the pew with his head in his hands mumbling to himself.

The nun was a sweet old lady. She came back with a pillow and two blankets. The pillow smelled like dust and coconut shavings, but it was soft. She told us goodnight before leaving Dad and I alone.

"Let's tuck you in," Dad stretched the blanket over me. The velvet of the pews felt rough against my skin, but it wasn't so bad. Dad tucked the blanket under my legs and arms like a cocoon. "There, all tucked in."

I giggled, the sound echoing faintly through the empty church. Though Dad smiled he looked sad. The dim light cast soft shadows against his face, sinking his eyes in further.

"Goodnight Dad," I said in a hushed whisper.

"Goodnight, get some rest," He ruffled my hair a bit before sitting down with a sigh. I studied him for a moment.

Dad's eyes were lined with dark eye bags and sunken in. His face looked like it had aged. Long deep wrinkles created long rivers in his skin. His hair was greasy and unkempt, and he still wore his wrinkled pajamas. His arms were covered in long red scratches and dark bruises discolored his skin.

Worry began to crawl into my throat. Its fingers were long and thin as they wove their way to my brain. I swallowed against the lump that had formed.

Is everything going to be okay?

<u>Nine</u>

"Okay, who's ready for recess?" Ms. Vera's voice was hoarse. She looked worn. The usual vibrant purples she wore seemed dull against her skin. Her knitted cardigan hung loosely around her thinning frame and her eyes were sunken in. Her cheeks were red and more pronounced while her hair lay tangled in a messy bun at the base of her neck.

The classroom erupted into small cheers, though everyone seemed a bit tired today. A classroom full of children was hard to wrangle already, but today they were fussy. I was the only one alert, finally having gotten some rest at the church last night.

"Alright but make sure to put your things back into your backpacks and push in your chairs please," She paused as a cough shook her body. "You can't go outside until your desks are clean."

She tucked a loose strand of hair behind her ear as she leaned against her desk. She closed her eyes for a minute, almost falling asleep. Her forehead and upper lip beaded with sweat and her body swayed slightly back and forth. Her cardigan fell gently from her right shoulder, exposing the strap of her tank top beneath.

A large purple and brown speckled bite mark indented her skin above her collarbone. The marks were red and raised around the edges where each tooth had torn at her skin. It looked painful to the touch.

"Ms. Vera?" A girl to my right spoke up against the clamoring of moving chairs and rustling bags. Our teacher opened her eyes slowly. She nodded for the girl to continue. "What happened to your shoulder?"

Ms. Vera's eyes widened. She scrambled to pull her cardigan up, her fingers getting caught in the thick knitted fabric. "It's nothing."

"It looks like it hurts," A boy chimed in. Ms. Vera's wide eyes moved quickly around the room, searching for a response.

"I visited a friend and their dog bit me," She waved a hand of dismissal. "It's no big deal. Let's go outside."

Everything was desolate. It was like the color had been drained out of the world. There were no birds flying through the sky or squirrels playing in the branches of the trees. It was empty. Not a single leaf lay on the branches of the surrounding trees. The grass was a brutish brown and yellow and broke at the slightest touch. The dirt was practically sand that released clouds of dust as everyone ran.

I stayed in the shade on the outskirts of the playground. Ms. Vera was slumped on the bench, her head tilted toward the sky and her eyes closed. Mr. Taylor stood close by as he worriedly adjusted his glasses.

My gaze fell to the ground where a single locust crawled between the blades of broken grass. Its body was plump and brown. Its antennae flicking back and forth as it walked. Black spots dotted its back and wings and its red eyes perched atop its head.

A crackling snapping sound pulled my attention. Another locust. Its brightly colored wings shifted through the air until they landed.

Then another.

And another.

And another.

I stood, my eyes flitting between each new one. But there were too many to keep up. I could feel fear winding its way through my body as my heart raced. A dark cloud surfaced from the ground just at the edge of the tree line. The snapping, crackling noises grew louder as the swarm approached, their bright yellow wings shimmering in the sunlight.

My body was frozen and my mind was a mess. I could feel my muscles twitching, begging me to run, but my eyes wouldn't turn away. The swarm swirled through the air, twisting and turning upon itself as they collided with the ground before springing back up. The sounds of their wings drew nearer, my lungs unable to breathe.

As the noise of their wings drowned out the surrounding environment it felt familiar. A sound I've heard before. It was something that overtakes everything else and blocks your ears. That grating, annoying sound.

The static.

I realized, it wasn't static at all. It was the swarm. I had been hearing the clacking of their wings as they drew near and now, they stood in front of me. Turning and undulating in a nauseating dance. My ears filled with the noise, my mind dizzy. The world swayed and then everything went black.

When I awoke my head felt as if it had been stuffed with cotton balls. My eyes burned as they floated lazily around the room. I could hear voices, muffled and hushed. I turned my head. My eyes landing on the pair. Dad and Ms. Vera stood by the door.

They looked upset, though I couldn't hear what they were saying. Dad's face was stern and his eyes dark. The corner of his eyes and forehead were lined with wrinkles. Ms. Vera looked frazzled. Her hands shook as she spoke, her expressions animated and angry. She hid her eyes with her hand as she listened to Dad.

He shook his head as he continued, waving an arm in my direction before pointing at himself.

Ms. Vera wiped at her nose, her body shuddering as she stood completely still. As the sleeve of her cardigan fell, I could see small red sores around her wrist.

Dad reached out to her, trying to move her hand from her eyes, but she slapped his hand away. She turned and walked away, storming out of the nurse's office.

Dad sighed as the door closed with a soft *click*. He looked even more exhausted than before. He wiped his eyes for a second, collecting himself.

"Hey," Dad's eyes met mine, lighting up as they did, a fake smile pushed against his lips. "How're you feeling? They told me what happened."

"I'm okay," I responded as I sat up. I felt far from okay. My entire body felt drained and weak. Every movement was heavy and lethargic. Dad clenched his jaw in the familiar way Mom would. I didn't meet his gaze.

"Okay," Dad patted the top of my head, smoothing out the hair and tucking it behind my ears. "Well, why don't we go home?"

I felt fear grab at me suddenly as my blood ran cold. "Do we have to?"

Dad's smile dropped. "Yeah-"

"Why? I don't want to go," Tears began to prick the back of my eyes. "Can we go back to the church?"

"No," He shook his head. "Mom is just sick is all. Everything will be fine I promise." He didn't even sound convinced by his own words. They felt empty and futile.

I could feel my heart beating against my chest, the sound of my pulse rushing through my ears. I felt dizzy again, but not in the way I did before. No this was a different kind of dizzy. This was the kind where nothing made sense, where my mind was moving to fast for me to comprehend, where fear crawled from my stomach into my throat.

"What about the church?"

"What about it? The priest was right, there is no such thing as demons," Dad gave me a sharp look. "I just wasn't thinking straight. Everything is fine."

Why do we have to go back?

Ten

The silence was uncomfortable. I found myself writhing in my seat, the soft clink of silverware against the plates was loud against my ears. It was deafening.

All three of us sat at the table, silence growing uncomfortably heavy in our ears. The tension in the air was palpable. Dad's muscles were tense and I could feel worry clawing at my throat. Mom was the only one who seemed calm, her demeanor unlike anything I'd seen from her before. It was…*uncanny*.

My stomach churned as I stared at the food. Chicken and rice. Something plain and simple, but it lacked flavor and the chicken was dry. Dad's cooking always came out like this. I pushed around a few pieces of rice with my fork. They slightly resembled maggots and for a second I felt bile rise in my throat. I looked up, studying my parents, trying to shake the image of maggots crawling from my mind.

My parents seemed to be interacting with one another normally enough, even though the color had drained from his face when we came home to Mom sitting on the couch.

"I wasn't a fan of the little rope trick you two pulled last night," Mom's voice was scratchy. Her eyes looked to Dad, but he refused to look up.

"Then maybe don't try to kill us when we're sleeping and we wouldn't have to," Dad said.

Mom began to laugh. It was a stuttering and shaky sound that shuddered her body and twitched her lips in an odd manner. "You're delusional."

"I'm delusional?" Dad scoffed. "I'm not the one acting insane in the middle of the night."

"Oh, please, I was just sleepwalking," Mom waved a hand of dismissal.

"Don't sit here and lie to me – to *us*," Dad pointed his knife between me and him.

"You want to talk about lying?" Mom set her utensils down, a warning tone in her voice. "Why don't we start with you? It's your favorite thing to do after all."

"What're you talking about?" Dad's knuckles turned white as he gripped the silverware.

"You know exactly what," Mom spat. "You never wanted any of this."

"Wanted what?" Dad's voice was cold.

"This. Us. Everything," She waved her hands through the air. "You didn't want to settle down. The only reason you even married me was because you didn't want to ruin your precious reputation by being an absentee-"

"That's enough," Dad cut her off, anger rising in the tone of his voice.

"Did you know that, Petra?" Mom turned to look at me, a fake smile spread across her lips. "Dad never wanted you. And he treated me like a hot piece of meat-"

"Enough," Dad pulled the napkin from around his neck. "You know none of that is true."

"All you saw in college was a nice slice of ass and you just had to get your grubby little paws on it."

"Terra-"

"You're nothing but a dog, is that why you bite so hard?"

"Terra enough."

"No, it's not. It's never enough for you, is it?"

"*Enough.*"

"You always want more, more, *more.*"

"You think I want more? Look! Look at what I've done for you," Dad waved his arms dramatically. "I gave up everything for you and your stupid little hobby."

"My job is not a hobby!" Mom slammed her hand into the table. "I never asked you to give up the luxurious life you so desperately needed to keep your dick up."

"What else was I supposed to do? Let you live out here by yourself for four years?"

"Yes! I'm an adult I can take care of myself and our child, of which you've neglected for the last three years."

"Neglected?" Dad's voice grew incredulously.

"Yes, N-E-G-L-E-C-T-E-D, *neglected.*"

"And you trying to break through her door at night is any better?"

"So, you admit it?"

"I didn't admit *shit*," Dad stood, his chair screeching as it shot out from under him, only to clatter on the floor. "I've had enough of this, and of you especially. All you do all day is dig in the dirt like some freak."

"Is that why you fuck her?"

Dad's eyes widened, his mouth agape. "Excuse me?"

"Is that why you spend every night in her bed away from your family?"

Dad shook his head as she continued. "One woman was never enough for you."

"That is enough," His voice deepened, a certain gruffness coming from his throat.

"So, is two enough? Or do you have a third you think I don't know about? Probably back home, right?" Mom tilted her head feigning thought. "What was her name? Cindy?"

"And what about you?" Dad slung his arm, his plate crashing to the ground. "Uprooting our entire lives for what? Some stupid piece of junk?"

Mom's face grew pale as he picked up the medallion. "Put it down."

"It's not even worth anything! Nobody reads your blogs or your books! Nobody gives a shit about you or your stupid occult nonsense!" He raised the medallion over his head, the metal gleaming in the light. "You're fucking worthless."

Time slowed as he brought his arm down, the medallion hurtling from his fingers. The metal shined in the light in flashes as it fell, the lion's head rotating, the legs spinning. It crashed to the ground, splintering into three fragments, denting the wood flooring.

"What have you done!?" Mom screamed. She crawled along the floor, cradling the broken pieces in her hands.

"Petra come here," Dad grabbed me by the wrist, pulling me from my seat.

Mom's ugly, dry sobs turned into that same stuttering, cackle from before. This time, however, it was heavier, sadistic. It crawled from deep within the base of her throat and fell against her yellow teeth and poisoned tongue.

My eyes remained on her as my feet tripped up the stairs, Dad's grip on my wrist tightening. Once we were at the top he let go grabbing me by the shoulders.

"Go get ready for bed," He tucked the hair behind my ears, his chest heaving. He started to move away.

"Do you love Mom?" The words blurted from my lips before I could stop them, like vomit when you're sick.

He stared at me for a long while. His lips were pursed and his eyes looked sad. "Things are complicated. You'll understand when you're older."

"Are you going to leave me here?" I asked. Every time I spoke, I swear I could see Dad flinch. It was as if a small jolt of electricity were being pushed through his chest and out his hands. His face would twitch, his expression pained.

"I would never," He sighed as he knelt back down. "Sometimes life gets messy. It doesn't always follow a set path and sometimes you don't know what path to take. I've been at a crossroad for a long time, or maybe a double lane highway, either way the point is, things get confusing and people get hurt–"

"So you don't love Mom anymore?" I interjected.

"No – I-I," He took a breath. "I don't know. I still have love for her, just things are different. People keep growing over time and things change."

I felt…confused. "You don't love me anymore?"

His face twisted. "God no, of course I love you. This only has to do with your mom and I...I promise."

None of Dad's responses really seemed to make sense to me, nor did I really understand the road references he was making, but I wasn't blind. The somber look on his face and the way his mouth would contort in subtle pain. He still cares for Mom, but there was no love there. There hadn't been for a long time. I would know. I saw it leave every night. I watched the affection die out like the embers of a fire. The way his hand would slip from Mom's in public, or when he'd walk ten feet ahead of us on the street. It was especially apparent when he wouldn't come home most nights. But I also knew if Dad ever left, he'd also leave me. Which means his words were empty.

"Okay," I said. A burning fire had begun in my chest. The heat formed a molten lump in my throat and my body felt weak.

"Go get ready for bed," He pushed me forward. "We're going to sleep in the living room tonight so hurry up."

"Can we build a blanket fort?"

"No, not tonight," Dad said as he walked toward the bathroom. I sighed. *We never get to do anything fun anymore.*

I was quick to brush my teeth and change into my pajamas, rushing with a newfound excitedness. Sleeping in the living room meant getting to watch TV late into the night. Dad would be none the wiser if I pretended I was asleep by squinting just enough so I could still see the screen through my lashes. I smiled a bit, until the conversation from earlier crept into my mind.

He's going to leave me here. I could feel it in my bones. It was a fact. Dad didn't want to move here, and he didn't care to pick me up most times. So, he would leave Mom and I on the side of the road like old luggage. Like he'd done before.

I stared out of my bedroom window. The sheep staring back at me. I felt a chill run down my spine. *Maybe he'd take me with him if I begged.*

<u>Eleven</u>

It wasn't as fun as I expected. Dad had put on an old western movie. The black and white pictures and old fake southern accents poured softly in the dim light of the living room.

My eyes wandered toward the stairs where Mom slept. The dark void of inky black shadows obscured the top from view. Dad and I had tied the door closed again tonight, though this time Mom didn't make any noise. My body shuddered suddenly

My eyes moved back toward the TV, the soft glow harsh against my tired eyes. I stole a glance at Dad.

His eyes were red at the edges, yet wide and alert. His pupils sat like pin pricks, barely visible against the blue of his irises. His hair was ragged and fell against his forehead in greasy strands. He almost looked like an entirely different person, wrought with age and worry. His jaw clenched as he crossed his arms, his eyes meeting mine.

"Go to sleep," His voice was softer than usual, almost apologetic. I watched as he turned back to the TV, not a single muscle in his body relaxing.

My eyes continued to traverse the rest of the house that remained shrouded in a tangled mess of gnarled shadows. The kitchen held an eerie yellow glow that emanated from the light above the stove. The light fell against the tiles, and flowed across the dining table, creating harsh lines against the wood grain of the chairs. Then my eyes caught it.

The medallion. The grimy light reflected against its smooth metallic surface, the glare making my eyes squint involuntarily. I could feel my heart begin to race. The world around me darkened, the shadows moving closer and closer, my vision focusing solely on that ugly piece of metal. Static filled my ears, blurring my thoughts and scrambling my mind. Whispers barely heard filtering through. I tried to hold onto the words, trying desperately to hear what they were saying, but the static was too loud, the house too dark.

My lungs burned and my throat tightened. It felt as though something had wrapped its fingers around my throat as something else pricked at my skin. A chill ran through my body as fear caressed my spine.

"This damn TV," My eyes snapped to Dad. He was pressing different buttons on the remote. My eyes flicked to the static filled screen. The darkness that once edged my vision was now gone. The screen flickered and returned to the western movie.

"I missed the best part." Dad groaned, setting down the remote in defeat.

My eyes moved back toward the kitchen where the yellow light of the stove seemed softer and shadows enveloped the dining room table. The medallion no longer glinting against the darkness. It was gone.

I let out a breath, feeling my eyelids grow heavy. I tried to focus on the movie Dad seemed so enthralled with but it was as if I no longer understood English. My mind was unable to focus, swaying back and forth between dreams and reality. The world warped and bent against itself, until it fell away entirely, lulling me into sleep's comforting embrace.

The rain woke me first. The sound of it rapping against the metal of the roof echoed through the house. It swirled with the howling wind and tapped against the windows in harmony with rustling branches.

My body felt restless as I sat up and rubbed the sleep from my eyes. I let out a groan as I sat up, my muscles aching.

Thump. I froze as ice pooled in my veins, suddenly wide awake. The sound came from above me, little bits of dust floating down through the air, the only evidence left of the noise. My eyes flicked to where Dad was next to me but were met instead with empty couch. I felt my breath hitch.

He abandoned me.

I turned to the TV in hopes of reprieve, but the black and white western was replaced by the void of static, the pixels flailing this way and that in complete and utter silence.

Thump.

This time louder. As my eyes dragged along the popcorn finish of the ceiling it started to grow dark. Oozing black mold spread out like a web. Long tendrils fanning out for three feet in every direction. The center of the mass was the darkest. It looked wet as it sagged against the ceiling, gravity desperate to release it from the sheet rock. I watched as a small drop built in the center, collecting within itself over and over. It grew until it began to shake against its own weight, begging to drop, taunting.

Thump.

The vibration from the thud upstairs sent the viscous drop tumbling to the ground, a long tendril of black lowering it before it snapped, allowing it to freefall. I moved closer pushing my body to the opposite end of the couch, leaning over the arm as far as I could. But it was dark. The molded liquid blended into the shadows. The white static of the TV cast just enough light to barely make out the edge of the droplet. As I moved closer, I was able to see the gleam of light was much larger than just the one drop. Instead, it was a congealed puddle. A mass of thick, dark, mold infested ooze from the ceiling.

I moved closer, reaching over the couch, my left hand sliding to find purchase on the side of the leather as my right hand crawled along the ground. My entire body was hanging over the side of the couch, my thighs sliding past the arm of it as my tippy toes pushed against the cushions.

I held my breath as I pushed myself further, my fingers mere inches away from the glob of ceiling run off.

Thunder crashed.

My heart jumped into my throat.

Panic surged through my heart.

Every muscle in my body contracted before I came crashing down along the floor, my head hit first, my shoulder twisted and my arm pinned beneath my hip at an awkward angle.

Dazed, I looked up the stairs. Ice shot through my veins.

"Mom?" My voice was a breathless whisper as I scrambled to sit up.

She stood near the top. Her hair matted and skin pulled taut against her cheeks. Her eyes wild and wide, reflecting the white TV static light back at me. She didn't move. Her white shirt hung loosely along her thin shoulders.

Silence fell between us for a few minutes, the only sound the rapping of the rain against the windows and roof. I refused to look away from her. Terrified that if I blinked for even a second, she would disappear – or *worse*.

My lungs burned, begging to release the breath I'd been unknowingly holding. I wanted to vomit from the effort.

I felt my heart race as she began to move. Her arms raised and hands placed gently onto the railing.

"*Mom*?" The word barely croaked from my throat. I felt the muscles in my body begin to ache, frozen, as fear coiled around my throat making it impossible to breathe.

She began to pull herself over the railing. Her thin frame moving unnaturally. The skin of her thighs sagged as she crouched along the rail. Her hair had fallen into her face.

I tried to back away, but my hand slipped, my elbow hitting the ground with a hallow *thud*. I winced.

I watched in terror as she began to move once more, reaching for the wall. Her fingers pressed into the sheetrock small streaks of white dust floating through the air as it cracked. Her feet followed next. Each movement was painstakingly slow, *deliberate*. She pulled herself along the wall leaving trails of dust and holes in her wake.

I could feel my pulse racing faster and faster.

She passed by the mold along the ceiling, taking a second turn her head and trail her tongue along the grotesque sagging liquid.

I felt tears trailing down my cheeks. Was I crying because I hadn't blinked? Or was I crying from fear? I couldn't tell.

She drew closer. Crawling impossibly silent as her face neared mine. Her head was now only a few feet from mine as she pushed herself away from the wall to hover just over me with the top half of her body.

I couldn't move. My body wouldn't. I was so terrified I was nearly turned to stone.

Now I could really see her. Her hair was thinned and tangled as it fell around her face and her shirt pooled along her shoulders exposing the rest of her bruised and torn skin. The flesh along her body looked mummified. It clung tight to her bones but sagged along her thighs and stomach. Large wrinkles dug deep through every part of her, even larger wounds covered in yellow pus and black ooze like that of the ceiling speckled her body like mold on food.

The smell.

It stung through my nose. It was putrid and pungent, slamming through my sinuses like a truck. I gagged, bile rising in my throat.

She pushed her face closer until I could hear her gurgled and labored breathing. Her face – *oh god* – her *face*.

The bags beneath her eyes pulled her bottom eyelids down so far the red of the skin was visible. The whites of her eyes were bloodshot and red, as if they were bleeding. The skin along her cheekbones looked as if it had been vacuum sealed to her skull. Sores covered her face and bruises gathered along her throat.

I felt a whine escape my lips. Sobs began to involuntarily wrack my body.

Her mouth pulled apart into a wide and crooked smile. Something was wrong. It was too wide and spread too far as her lips began to crack and bleed. Black ooze covered her yellowed and rotted teeth.

She pushed her head closer to mine, our foreheads nearly touching. The sound of the rain had long since been drowned out by the sound of my own pulse hammering in my ears.

She let out a breathless hiss. Hot moist air radiated towards me. The smell putrid as it hit my face. Hot tears raced down my cheeks as bile rose in my throat.

I couldn't look away. My eyes were glued to hers. My mother. But it wasn't her. It couldn't be. Her eyes were red and oozing, her mouth far too wide. My entire body was numb, a rush of static filled my ears. Fear tore at the very essence of my soul, its long, sharp claws dug desperately through my body and coiled around my throat.

I tried to scream but no sound escaped as she drew closer. She almost seemed to pull me closer, drawing me in as her mouth grew wider, her teeth skewed and crooked. I could see down her throat, a mangled mess of guts and puss. Strings of saliva tearing and dripping, hitting gently against my cheeks as her teeth scraped over the crown of my head, my vision going dark.

Her head snapped suddenly, teeth grinding across my skull. I let out the breath I had been holding. Her body was paused above mine watching the door.

My fingers began to slide back, trying to pull my body away from her unnoticed. I let out a yelp as she scuttled quickly back across the wall and ceiling. Her body moved inhumanly fast her joints at odd angles, dust trailed through the air after her. She disappeared beyond the void of the staircase just as I heard the '*click*' of the front door lock.

I couldn't move. Just turned my eyes to watch as the door slid open, quietly, softly as if it too wished to be unnoticed. My entire body shook, the static having faded.

Dad stepped through the door, removing his shoes and placing his keys on the rack, streaks of rain fell along his jacket. His eyes met mine.

"Petra?"

I could feel snot roll down my upper lip, but I didn't dare to move.

"What're you doing up?" His tone was accusatory. As if he wanted to scold me for being awake. As if I wasn't supposed to see him walking through the door.

He came closer, eyeing me cautiously. His eyes flicked up to the stairway, then down to me. "Get up, what did you get all over yourself?"

He pulled me up by the elbow, his jacket leaving little droplets of rain along my skin. It was only then that I looked down at my hands. That disgusting, slimy mold coated both of them. It was even under my nails somehow.

I didn't respond. My hands trembled, my legs shook, and the top of my head burned. *This has to be a dream. I'm going to wake up any minute.*

"Go wash your hands and come lay back down, you have school tomorrow," He pushed a hand against my back, ushering me to the kitchen. So, I did as I was told.

Twelve

The world seemed devoid of life. The branches of the trees were bare, their trunks and limbs shining a dull grey in the pale sunlight. The grass was brittle, the crunch of it loud against my feet. Everything looked…*dead.*

Normally when it rains the world seems to be more vibrant, more *alive*. Instead, it felt like the rain had washed away what little resources had existed to feed the plants in the first place. I looked down.

The mud stuck to my shoes. The color stained red from the clay as it suctioned itself to me, trying to tug my shoes from my feet as I trudged along. It was chunky and thick, curling into my shoelaces and along the edge of my frilly pink socks. It reminded me of the mold from last night. The way it sloughed off my shoes and clung to it.

My eyes trailed up the water sodden grass that somehow remained brittle, until it stopped against the divet. I don't know why I always made my way toward it. Almost every recess. Originally, I thought it would eventually fill up with dirt on its own. As if the wind would push the dirt into it, or maybe ants would believe it to be a great start to their home, less digging they had to do. But it always remained empty.

Except for today. I felt my heart jump, a small pang of excitement opening my eyes. Rushing over I could see them, just barely under the murky water surface. Their little bodies swishing this way and that, kicking up more and more mud. I smiled. *Tadpoles*.

I waved a hand at them, stifling a giggle as they ran and hid from my shadow. They were cute. As I stared, a feeling started to build in my stomach before bubbling up in my throat. I wanted to protect them. Somehow, someway I felt mildly responsible. This was my little divet of earth and I had been waiting for something to happen and here it was. I had asked for it, therefore they were my responsibility. Besides it's not like the mama frog would be back to help. *I think*.

I charged toward the edge of the woods, teetering on one foot as I reached down to pick up a few of the stones. I pulled my shirt away from me and piled them into it like a makeshift basket. I tried to collect the prettiest ones. Stacking them gently against each other until they grew so heavy my shirt was stretched out from the weight.

I waddled back, hugging the rocks close. Once at the edge of the pool of tadpole infested waters, I squatted down and began the tedious process of gently brushing off each rock and setting it around the edge. I knew the tadpoles would eventually turn into frogs and need to get out of the water, so I dipped my hand into the warm water and dug a small ramp for them to use later. I was careful not to disturb the dirt too much, watching swirling patterns of it kick up as the tadpoles ran desperately away from me.

"I'm not going to hurt you, I promise," I cooed at them. My hand hesitated over the murky water for a second. My fingers twitched and my eyes darted back and forth.

Something seemed to take hold of me. I felt this undeniable urge to scoop one out, to feel it squirm in between my fingers, to squeeze it gently and feel it pop –

Static began to build in my ears, the whispers of voices unintelligible. My hand pushed into the water reaching toward the slowest one. My eyes followed its movements, cornering it against the wall of mud it was trapped in. The static grew louder as my hand began to close, my vision growing dark at the corners.

I blinked. Ripping my hand from the water I felt my lungs burning. Guilt tore through me, my mind swirling with confusion. I don't want to hurt them so why?

"I'm sorry," I felt tears building behind my eyes. I watched the tadpole I had trapped, meet with the others and sink into the shadows. "I'm so sorry. I didn't mean to."

"What're you doing?" Autumn stared at me. Her arms were crossed over her chest. She wore a white sleeveless shirt with ruffles along the shoulders. It tucked into a pleated black skirt. Her black flats had mud along the sides but her ruffled white socks were perfectly clean.

"Nothing," I didn't dare to look back at the divet, nor the embarrassing amount of rocks cradled in my dirtied shirt.

"Why're you covered in mud if you're not doing anything?" Lea chimed in. Her long hair was tied back into a french braid. She wore an oversized blue pinstriped dress shirt and khaki shorts. Her white trainers were also somehow nearly perfectly clean. There was only a small bit of mud on the top of her right shoe.

My eyes trailed down to my stretched-out and mud-covered shirt and my equally dirty hands. I felt embarrassed.

"She really looks like a dog now," Ivy snorted. Her white headband shown bright against her blonde hair. Speaking of, her hair swayed gently at the edges as a small breeze tugged and tangled its way through it.

My eyes darted down to her pristine white socks peaking over her pretty pink sneakers. Pearls and bows adorned it like decorated medals and trophies.

"What's this?" Autumn stepped closer, bending down and putting her hands on her knees. Her eyes widened as she spotted them. All of them. My tiny friends I felt so compelled to protect.

"Oh my…*gosh*." Ivy leaned down before laughing and grabbing at her stomach. I felt my heart drop.

"You're kidding." Lea gasped. The end of her braid fell over her shoulder as she leaned forward.

Autumn stood, kicking a rock into the pool, the tadpoles scattered.

"Stop!" I yelled, pushing her legs. Her foot slipped in the mud, her knees buckled, and down she fell. There was a wet *squelch* sound as she pushed herself up.

"What is wrong with you?" She shrieked. Her eyes were wild like a fire. I could hear my pulse in my ears. She leapt at me, pushing me into the ground. I could feel the cold of the slick mud as it pressed into my shirt and hair. I struggled against her pushing at her arms and face. "Grab her!"

I felt two sets of hands wrap around the crook of my elbows. My arms flailed wildly, my legs kicking out at Autumn, my right foot connecting with her gut. She let out a gasp, reeling back.

"Look at what you did!" She motioned at her clothes; her face covered in half dried mud. Some of it was stuck between her teeth. The corner of my mouth twitched up as if to smile.

"What do we do now?" Ivy whined. Her hands slipped against my skin from the mud. I watched as Autumn's eyes flicked between the girls and mine. Then they landed on the pond.

I looked past her, hoping to catch Ms. Vera's eye. I scanned quickly over the other kids running, laughing and playing, then I spotted her. But she was busy talking to Todd near the benches.

"I have an idea." Autumn's voice pulled my eyes back to her as she reached into the pool of water and grabbed a tadpole.

"Put it back." My voice was louder than I expected.

Autumn smiled. "No." She pinched the tail between her two fingers and held it up. Its wriggling slimy body fought to be free of her grasp. "Open her mouth."

Ivy did as she was told, releasing my right arm and pushing her fingers into my mouth. It was disgusting. Her fingers tasted like nail polish and dirt. I bit at her fingertips while trying to wrestle my other arm free from Lea. Autumn approached with the tadpole, held just above my head.

Time seemed to slow. The air began to whisper, like an unseen chorus of voices constantly overlapping one another in an uncomprehensible language. The very sounds of the world frayed at the edges, splitting, as if I were somehow caught between the stations of different realities. My vision darkened at the edges, a slow pool of shadows homing in on the small creature above me.

Its slimy body had started to grow cold from the outside air, thick mucus trying desperately to keep it alive until returned to the water.

Autumn's malicious smile sat blurry in the background. She looked like my mother did last night. That almost too wide smile. But she had perfect teeth.

My mouth was forced open. The tadpole drew closer. The noise of the world was lost to me. I couldn't hear anything they were saying but I was sure they were laughing. Their high pitched nasally laughs would haunt me across the playground or in the classroom. I could never escape them.

My right hand, which had still been barely successful in staying out of Lea's grasp, landed on something cold and hard. Autumn grabbed my shirt and my legs stopped kicking. My entire body became numb. My fingers coiled around the edges of the rock, feeling the grooves along my fingertips, feeling its weight in my palm.

Autumn grew closer. Ivy's fingers pulled away but a few remained just to hold my mouth still as she gripped my chin. Lea had wrapped an arm around my chest, hugging me to her to stop my previously wild movements. The whispering static buzzed and hissed, the chanting whispers growing louder and more desperate. My vision nearly completely black leaving only a small tunnel to view the innocent creature in all of this losing its life.

I swung.

My right arm flew through the air. The impact was jarring, vibrating down my entire arm. My mouth suddenly slammed shut as Autumn crumpled to the ground. Ivy screamed. A loud piercing, almost animalistic sound. Everyone looked.

"Oh my god, oh my god!" Lea let go pushing me away as I spat. My spit was red. Blood and saliva mixed together in a swirling bubbled mess, but there was more. A small fingertip and a much larger piece of finger. I gagged.

My eyes landed on the tadpole. Motionless. Its body suspended in that disgusting mud. I poked at it. It didn't move. My eyes stung. I picked it up gently, placing it back in the shallow pool of water. The others swam away from me, darting into the shadows, terrified.

The body of the lifeless one sank to the bottom. The sunlight draping over it and reflecting along the bottoms edge. A small cloud of dust swirling around it. Tears began to fall from my eyes, rippling against the water's surface. My reflection was impossible to see.

"Petra!" Ms. Vera never yells. Not normally. I turned to look at her. She looked worried. Her skin was pale, almost a ghostly color. Her veins thinly veiled just below her skin. Her hair was thin and stringy, much different from how it looked before. It was tied back in a bun against the nape of her neck. She wore a long sleeve black turtleneck under a deep purple cardigan. Her purple leather boots were covered in thick mud. Her arms were crossed, hugging tightly to her thin frame.

Her eyes flicked to Autumn on the ground. "What have you done?!" Her voice was shrill and panicked. My eyes fell back to the pool of water. The lone tadpole still laid bare against the ground, the light no longer shining down. It looked peaceful.

I didn't have an answer. Nothing but silence and echoed whispers filtered through my ears as the wind slowly clawed at my reflection in the water. There was nothing to say.

Thirteen

"I apologize," Dad looked upset. Not the kind of upset where he'd leave the house when arguing with Mom. This was the kind where his jaw tightened. His eyes were dark and intense. He was mad.

"Look, Sir, we believe she should be suspended for a few days," The principal was calm. A man about the size of Dad. But his hair was darker and salted with sprinkles of grey. He had deep lines in his forehead from raising his eyebrows.

"Suspended?"

"Sir, I don't mean to be rash, but she knocked a kid out with a rock," The principal leaned forward placing his hands, fingers intertwined, in front of him. "And she bit the fingertips off another."

He whispered the last part. Not a quiet kind of whisper that withholds information, but instead the kind that tries to emphasize it. Dad gritted his teeth, hanging his head in defeat.

"I understand."

"The parents decided not to press charges," The principal continued. "Considering a few students have come forward stating they initiated the struggle. I would say being suspended would be good for her. Get some time at home. Let things cool off over here."

"Yeah," Dad nodded. "I agree."

The door slammed shut. The house was quiet. The floorboards didn't groan, the stairs didn't creak, and the TV remained off.

"Go put your stuff down, then come sit at the table," His voice was stern but as I looked at him there was something else in his eyes. Something that made the veins in his neck pop and all his muscles overly tense. If you painted him grey people would think he was a statue with how cold and rigid he looked.

I stared at him for a second. Watching him as his eyes scanned the shadows of the house.

"Go on," He pushed a hand against my back, ushering me forward.

I walked. One tentative step in front of the other. The groan of the floorboards was loud against my shoes. I felt on edge. Every fiber of my being waiting for something to jump out of the shadows at me. Nothing came.

I reached the top of the stairs. The silence was loud. Deafening. My eyes flitted across the walls and carpet. All the doors were closed. I waited a bit longer, straining my ears to hear anything, but there were none.

I bolted. Sprinting toward the door to my room I could feel the panic in my legs. I held my breath, shoving the door open just wide enough to throw my bag into it. I turned, half expecting Mom to be there, but she wasn't. Empty hallway greeted my eyes. I tore down the stairs, stumbling, my foot catching where the carpet met the wood. When I got there

Dad was sitting at the table. His hands crossed like the principal had earlier. He stared out the window.

As I drew near, I could see it. Mom stood in the middle of the yard where the sheep were kept. They stood in a circle around her, their eyes fixated on her as she spread her arms out wide. Long black veins traced across her arms, and her hair was nearly gone. What was left was stringy and tangled.

"Sit down," My eyes connected with Dad's. He looked worried. I did as I was told. "We need to talk about what happened at school today." Though his tone was cold his voice still wavered.

"Okay."

"Do you understand the gravity of what you've done today?"

"Yes," I watched him as his eyes made their way back to Mom.

"I don't think you do," He turned to me. "Those two little girls are in the hospital because of you." He pointed a finger at me.

"They bullied me," My voice was small.

"I know you're saying they bullied you, but that doesn't warrant what you did. You can't go around beating people up just because you think they're being mean to you."

"They were though," I crossed my arms.

"I don't give a damn if they teased you at school. That doesn't give you the right to do what you did, *Petra*." He sounded exasperated.

"They were trying to make me eat it," I pleaded, my voice high and whiny.

"Eat what?"

"The tadpole," I felt tears sting the back of my eyes. Memories flashed through my mind of the way it wriggled in Autumn's fingers. The way they laughed and smiled. "They tried to make me eat it."

"God, Petra. Suck it up. It's not that big of a deal and I doubt that's even true," He threw his arms out. "Why don't you tell me what really happened?"

"I'm telling you the truth," I more mumbled it than spoke. The words barely got past my lips.

"Do you really think I'm going to believe a group a girls tried to antagonize you into eat a fucking tadpole?"

"It's true!"

"It's not and you know it!"

"Dad!"

"Petra–"

"They started it!" I stood up from my chair, the screeching of its wooden legs on the kitchen tile loud against my ears.

"Sit down!" He slammed a hand on the table. "That is *enough*. This is ridiculous. You're acting like your mother." He shook his head.

"Dad, *please*," I begged. The tears now fell from my eyes, running down my cheeks.

"Grow the fuck up," He pointed at me again. "Quit crying. Do I need to give you something to cry about?"

"N-no sir," I choked out.

"Then that's enough. You sent two girls to the hospital today," Dad leaned back in his chair. "You did that. I didnt raise you to act like a selfish entitle brat."

I just cried. For the first time in a long time, I really and truly cried. It was uncontrollable. My body was wracked with sobs, everything in me finally released. I didn't know I had been holding in so much. I could feel all the emotions from the week pouring through me at once. Anger and hatred, exhaustion and fear, everything intertwined into a massive ball of pain and sorrow.

I didn't want to be in the house anymore. I didn't want to be getting yelled at by Dad. I didn't want to hurt those tadpoles. I didn't want Mom to be acting weird. I hated it. I hated it. I *hated* it.

"They deserved it!" The words came out like vomit, surprising even me. I felt my heart drop. I had meant those words, I knew I did, and yet the look on Dad's face made me regret ever uttering them.

"What did you just say?" His tone was condemning. His eyebrow raised, his eyes locked entirely onto mine.

"I didn't..." My voice trailed off. My tears had stopped.

"Enough!" Dad ripped the vase from the table, hurling it across the room into the wall. It shattered upon impact followed by the clattering of the shards falling along the ground. I held my breath. I was unable to move. Fear began to press its long claws against my throat, a lump formed there. "Go to your room."

I looked out the window. Mom was still standing there. The sheep were moving around her in a circle in three rings.

Those closest to her moved clockwise, the next ring moved counterclockwise, and the next moved clockwise, and so on. The pattern repeated until all the sheep were moving around her, dust kicking up at their feet. I could hear one sheep in particular. It kept bleating, growing louder and more pained. I couldn't see it but could tell it was close to the center where Mom stood. Her back was to the window, but I could still make out her thin frame against her robe and the yellow outside light of the dying sun.

"I said to go to your room," Dad repeated.

I stood from the table, taking one more quick glance at Mom before trudging upstairs.

The shower water didnt help to calm my emotions at all. I always see characters in movies feeling better after a warm shower, but it just didn't seem to be working. Maybe I didn't have the water warm enough, or *was it too warm*?

I shook my head. *It doesn't matter*. I changed into my pajamas and left the bathroom. The doors were still closed to both the spare bedroom and my parents' room. I went down the first couple of stairs, peaking down to see if Dad was still home. I knew he wasn't. I had heard and felt the vibrations of the walls as he started his car when I was in the shower. I just hoped it wasn't true. I sighed as fear wound its way back up my body once again.

I made my way back to my room and began preparations to the best of my ability. I knew that at night

Mom sometimes got worse. Whatever sickness was enveloping her was progressing and after last night I wasn't taking any chances.

I pressed my back against the edge of my dresser, pushing with my legs as hard as I could. It was slow going but eventually it was snug against the door. The handle just above the top of it. If someone tried to open the door it would be nearly impossible.

But just in case...I pushed both night stands up against the dresser. They were much easier to move. Then I began to drag my bed. I was growing lightheaded as I pulled it along. It felt impossible and I was exhausted, but I knew there was no way I would be able to sleep if I didn't feel safe.

Safe was relative.

I don't think I had felt safe for a single moment in the last week. With everything that was happening my mind was constantly spinning. Between school and my parents...Dad was always gone, but that wasn't unusual, and Mom was sick. It was all so confusing. I couldn't make sense of it.

Dad is a doctor so why doesn't he fix her?

To tell the truth, I don't think he wants to. I think sometimes he hopes Mom will just disappear. That one day he wouldn't have to come back to her...or me. He didn't want to help Mom because he couldn't. If she got better, he would be forced to stay. I knew that he wouldn't. Maybe if he moved in with Ms. Vera, he would take me over there too.

Mom isn't bad. I reminded myself. *Just sick*. I felt myself growing angry. Dad should just fix her. Take her to the hospital where he works and fix her. Be the good Dad that I remembered before we moved.

The floor was hard against my back and hips. My pillow did little to cushion my head, and my comforter felt oddly too large as it sprawled across the ground around me. I had grabbed as many stuffed animals as I could, gathering them around me like Mom did the sheep.

I tried to stay awake for as long as possible, but my eyes grew heavy and my body felt so warm. Granted, I didn't have any real faith in my barricade. Yet, sleep hugged me close, lulling me deeper...and deeper.

My eyes snapped open. Sweat clung to my entire body. It was hot, too hot. I flung the comforter off as my eyes jerked to the door. It was still closed and my barricade was just how I left it.

That wasn't why I woke up. No. It was the noise. Incessant howling and chanting. It flooded through my ears and crawled into the corners of my mind. I stood, running to the window. The sight before me was both horrifying and incredible.

Fire rose nearly six feet into the air. It roared and burned, eagerly eating at the wood and sticks sacrificed to it. The bones and flowers we had dug up were scattered around the outer edge of the procession. The sheep circled around Mom who stood in the center once again. This time they moved faster. They were nearly sprinting at full speed around her. The chaos was...*intoxicating*.

I couldn't avert my eyes. The flames were too bright, and yet my eyes were wide open, watching as they licked at the open air, small sparks flying in every direction. The sheep bleated as they ran, begging for mercy. They couldn't stop. Their hooves were keeping an unholy, eternal beat as Mom was chanting. *Mom*?

She was naked, dancing around the fire in a whirlwind of movement. The shadows where the light of the fire couldn't reach would trace along her body. Almost every bone was visible, deep bruises and dying wounds covered her flesh. She was sweating profusely, dripping down her face and arms as she swayed back and forth. She raised her hands, twirling to face the window. I held my breath.

A lamb was clutched in her hands. It looked so cute and frail. She smiled. That crooked, yellow smile that was somehow too wide. Her eyes reflected the light like a cat's, shining bright green as she watched me. She held the lamb up higher over her head. Its fur was still tinged a slight red from its recent birth. A small smile tugged at the corner of my mouth. Its ears were far too big for its head.

Mom chanted a few more words, her eyes never left mine. She lowered the lamb to her face, kissing it on the forehead. My lungs burned in anticipation. I was both confused and transfixed. The whispering was back, growing louder. It sounded so similar to the chanting Mom was doing only seconds ago. It filled my ears until I could hear nothing else. The sheep spun and spun in horrible circles. The fire grew taller and taller, trying to lick at the branches of the trees above were the little wax sealed papers hung.

Mom held the lamb close to her face, her smile grew wider, *larger*.

CRUNCH.

My body went cold. My stomach lurched. Mom laughed, blood spilled from her mouth, one of those too large ears flopped against her bottom lip. The head. The head of the lamb. She just...*bit it*. With sickening sounds of crunching and wetness, she continued to chew. She swallowed it down before her teeth clamped down once more.

My legs buckled. I felt hot tears trace my cheeks. Bile stuck in my throat, the static chant of unintelligible voices started to die down, my vision grew blurry. My stomach burned. It felt like the fire that was outside was suddenly inside. Everything twisted and hurt.

I wiped my brow, my sleeve soaked when I pulled it away. My breathing was erratic, my lungs burned as if I had inhaled smoke. I coughed. Coughing made it worse. The pain wouldn't stop. It kept building, like someone was holding a hot knife against my stomach. I tried to move but failed.

My hands and feet slipped across the floor. My right arm gripped my stomach while the other tried to pull me across the floor. Due to the sweat I slid more than moved.

I let out a scream. It was something guttural and vulgar. I just wanted it to end. The pain was impossible to bear. I could hear her laugh outside, the image of the lamb unable to leave my mind. I was reminded of the tadpole and how innocent it was, then the lamb and how cute it had been. The way both had met such gruesome ends, and yet I was still here. The pain was immeasurable.

I gagged, choking against my own breathing as if my lungs couldn't decide whether to breath in or out. I screamed again out of desperation. *Am I going to die?*

Tears streamed down my face mixing with the salty taste of sweat against my skin. My fingertips brushed against one of the bed posts. My nails dug into soft paint and even softer wood. It collected under my nails. There was no way I could move this.

My entire body was aflame. Synapses and nerves firing on all cylinders. My mind felt like the pool of tadpoles, turbulent and murky. If someone were to shove me into the fires of hell, this is what I imagined it felt like.

God help me.

I wasn't religious, at least not that I remembered. Maybe if God did exist, he would stop it. Maybe if I begged enough, he'd come to my aid. He could perform miracles, right? Why not save me? I'm still his child, aren't I? Or am I punished because I didn't attend Sunday school all those years ago when Mom asked? Is God abandoning me like Dad?

My flesh seared as screams echoed from my throat. My lips were flaked and red as tears strewn with blood fell from my eyes. My throat was hoarse, my voice nearly gone, and yet I begged.

Please.

It wasn't enough. Crooked fingers cloaked in soot closed together in empty prayer as the skin of my knees tore from the bone while I pushed myself up to kneel. My muscles screamed in agony as my lungs heaved with effort. Words I couldn't understand, mumbled and coarse fell from my mouth in barely a whisper.

Dad. Please. Help me.

Small embers filled my arms and legs as if I were kindling. Dancing yellow flames erupted around me. My hands pushed at the fire trying desperately to stamp it out, but with each swing of my arm another ember would ignite. Skin sloughed off as I pulled myself across the floor. There would be no hand to pull me up. There would be no savior donned in shining armor. I was alone.

My stomach wretched and ripped the vomit from my gut. I couldn't tell if I was vomiting from the pain or otherwise. It smelled horrible and looked so close to the mold from before. It spilled out across the floor and there was nothing I could do. So, I let it consume me. If I were to burn, then I would do so.

Fourteen

It was Tuesday when I was given at home suspension. With how Ivy and Autumn were doing, the principal had called Dad to explain I should remain home for a bit longer, as things hadn't quite cooled off as he'd expected. It has been over a week since the incident.

Turns out Ivy couldn't hold any food down. They think I traumatized her so badly she's got PTSD. Autumn still hasn't woken up, but they were saying she'd lost all her hair and developed a rash. Lea has become mute. She refuses to speak and when she does the words aren't formed right and her sentences are mixed up.

Their parents are really upset, rightfully so. The principal had asked how I was doing. Dad had said I was fine. He didn't tell him about the condition he found me in just a few nights ago. He preferred to lie. To be honest, I didn't really want to talk about it either. Everything was really blurry.

I remember the fire, Mom, the lamb, and throwing up, but it all was so hazy I couldn't tell if I had dreamt it. I probably would've taken it to be a nightmare if I hadn't seen the charred grass that remained. My eyes traced the path the sheep had ran examining all the dents and hoof prints.

"Petra," Dad's voice called from the driveway. I stared at the charred grass one more time before looking at the sheep. They were acting completely normal. "Petra come on, you're going to be late."

That night was all I could think about, and yet Dad didn't seem to want to think about it at all. I don't really know how he managed to get into my room. Only that he did. He found me lying in a puddle of my own puke, cold and pale. He apologized a lot that morning. His eyes were red and puffy. When he asked what happened, I just shrugged.

How could I ever explain that to him?

He didn't even believe me about the tadpole, so it didn't really matter. He would never believe me about this. I kept my lips sealed.

And Mom? He had asked. I just shrugged again.

After I passed out, I had no idea what Mom did. The house was quiet and the sheep were back to normal. Maybe she disappeared like Dad seemed to want so badly. I would be lying if I said I hadn't hoped that was a possibility. Instead, he found their bedroom door stuck shut. We both assumed she was in there. That's where she stayed for the next few days.

Dormant. He had said. Like some parasite that goes into hibernation. I didn't know if that was a thing. Dad rambled about incubation periods, nothing that I could really understand though.

I would've liked to believe I could relax during this dormant period, but it made me feel even more on edge. Something about the house being silent every single night was off putting. Maybe I had just grown so used to stress my body could no longer relax. Sleeping was nearly impossible. Nightmares would torment me if my eyes sought to close. I couldn't get the image of the lamb out of my mind. It made me sick.

Today is Wednesday. I kept repeating it to myself. If I kept track of the days, I felt less like I was going crazy. I'd had a headache since the bonfire Mom decided to throw. I didn't want to tell Dad but told myself if it didn't go away by tomorrow I would. My body still felt a bit sore and my throat was still hoarse from puking. But I was alive.

Maybe God had performed a miracle. It sure felt like I was going to die that night, and here I was, still alive. Though it didn't feel like a miracle. It felt like anything but. I couldn't shake this intense dread that seemed to marinate in my bones. It was heavy and oppressive, like one of those heated, weighted blankets they give to elderly people in nursing homes. Except the heat was set too high and the weight was too heavy. It made my bones feel like they were melting.

"I need you to behave today, please," Dad's voice was quiet. It didn't hold that same strength and cold tone I had grown so accustomed to.

I nodded.

"I'll pick you up from school today, alright?" He glanced at me as he parked. "We can stay down in the living room together tonight and build a blanket fort. Does that sound like fun?"

I wouldn't look at him. My head hurt too much, and the sun was too bright. He waited a bit longer for a response.

"Alright, well I'll see you this afternoon," He unlocked the car. Accepting the silence I was providing. I opened the door and left, not bothering to look back.

Mr. Taylor was his usual self. Scrawny and pale with a neat kept tweed suit. It looked perfectly ironed and sat loose across his boney shoulders. He wrung his hands as he spoke, his voice barely carrying across the room.

I sat in the back. Every now and then one of my classmates would turn and watch me from the corner of their eyes. I stared straight ahead, pretending not to notice them. Whispers would swim through them like a small school of fish warning each other about the shark looming nearby.

But I wasn't a shark. I didn't think so at least. Or maybe I was and Dad was right, I am just like Mom.

"Each star is an important part of the universe," Mr. Taylor pointed at the map of the solar system he had projected across the chalkboard. It was blurry and hard to read. The projection filtered over him, mapping the stars across his skin as if he were a part of it. "Each of you are made of stardust."

"Or black holes," Jake said. He was taller than most of the other boys. He liked to call himself the class clown, self-proclaimed of course. He snickered as his eyes met mine.

"Well black holes are sometimes formed by the collapse of massive stars," Mr. Taylor pushed his glasses up nervously. "There is beauty even in darkness."

A hand shot up. "Yes Dolly?"

"What about signs?" Dolly was the smartest girl in school. She always carried around large books and never seemed to run out of pencils.

"Signs?" Mr. Taylor tugged at his fingers, digging each nail under the other.

"Yeah like, ya know, pieces and lions," Dolly nodded her head. Mr. Taylor's brow furrowed before his hands stopped.

"Do you mean astrological signs? *Pisces* and *Leo*," He cautiously corrected.

"Yes, those," Dolly replied eagerly.

"Ah, yes," Mr. Taylor walked toward his desk at the front middle of the room and sat on the stool. "Astrological signs are believed to carry great significance. Depending on your time and place of birth you can be attributed to one of twelve different signs."

"What sign are you Mr. Taylor?" Peggy spoke up.

"I believe I'm a Virgo," Mr. Taylor wrung his hands a bit more. Sweat began to build along his brow, but he quickly wiped it away.

"What's does a Virgo do?" Chad this time.

"To tell you the truth, I'm not entirely sure."

"What about the years?" Casey now.

"The years?"

"Yeah," Casey nodded. "Don't the years have signs?"

"Years don't have birthdays," Jake again.

"Actually," Mr. Taylor pushed up his glasses. "Casey is correct. The years run through the cycle of the signs."

"When was this year born?" Jonah asked.

"Years don't have birthdays, idiot," Jake's voice sounded frustrated.

"No name calling Jake," Mr. Taylor warned. "The year may not have a birthday, but the signs do have seasons. I believe we are currently in the season of..."

His voice trailed off as he looked at his phone. His fingers flew frantically across the screen. He took a pause as he read to wipe at his brow. He looked paler than before. As if he was somehow draining of color. The projector light that shone across his thinning hair didn't help. *Was his hair always thin*?

"Sagittarius," Mr. Taylor looked up as he put his phone away. "We're in the season of Sa-Sagi-Sagittarius." His voice seemed to catch in his throat. He coughed. It sounded hoarse as if his lungs were made of sandpaper. As he cleared his throat I felt a wave of exhaustion creep over me. My eyes felt heavy, closing slower and slower. A buzzing filled my ears. Small voices and whispers piling over one another as if desperate to be heard first. My heart seemed to beat harder but slower, each beat more intentional than the last.

"Sorry," Mr. Taylor choked on the words. "One-one s-second." He held up a finger, his eyes burned with fear. His greying hair stuck to his forehead as rivulets of sweat ran down his face, tinting his suit darker.

"Mr. Taylor...are you okay?" Casey asked tentatively.

"I'm f-fine," He tried to stand but his legs buckled. He caught himself sweat dripping between his hands as his eyes stared at the table. He mumbled something under his breath.

"What?" Jake stood from his chair, craning his neck forward to hear better. Everyone held their breath.

"Sagit-" He chewed at his tongue. "Sagittar-sag...sagit...sag..."

The static spiked, the chanting drowned out the rest of the room, but my eyes wouldn't leave him. His head twitched and his entire body shook. Images of Mom and the sheep flashed against my eyes. The shrill buzzing of a million bees coursed through my ears. My head was pounding. It felt like my heart was failing and my lungs burned. *When was the last time I breathed*?

I couldn't tell. Mr. Taylors mouth opened and closed like a fish out of water. His hands clawed at the table, his nails scraping against the wood. He yanked at his lanyard, the thin ribbon-like fibers tearing into his skin. His eyes met mine.

"Sagittarius."

THUNK!

The entire class reeled back. A long string of dark red blood fell lazily from Mr. Taylor's forehead and fell to the desk. Tears streamed down his cheeks. A large gash filled his forehead from the impact. Everyone stayed still.

THUNK!

THUNK!

THUNK!

He continued. His head crashed into the desk repeatedly. Blood poured from his face as he did. His nose gave way first. It broke and splintered across his cheeks. My classmates screamed and ran from the room, trampling over one another in the process.

I couldn't move. My entire body was screaming at me to run, but I was stuck. Every time he'd raise his head, his face more and more mangled, his eyes would lock onto mine. I watched as his teeth gave way next. They spilled from his mouth with pieces of his gums. Blood and saliva became one and covered his desk. He cried. Sobs tore through his body as if he were praying. He choked and gurgled against the blood and spit.

"Oh my god!" Ms. Vera ran into the room, phone in hand. She grabbed him by the shoulders trying to stop him, but it continued. She couldn't stop it. The beat of his head against the desk was eternal and unnerving. The static rose into a chant and grew faster with every passing second.

Like the static in my ears, he began to slam his head down faster. The pace was horrifying. His arms were slack at his side, his body hinging at the hips.

Ms. Vera was yelling but I couldn't hear her. She waved her arms at me, but I ignored her. It wasn't like I could move anyway. I was stuck. Like how I was stuck watching Mom with the lamb, how I was stuck watching Autumn draw the tadpole closer, and how I was stuck when Mom tried to eat me.

In a desperate attempt, Ms. Vera tore her cardigan off and placed it in front of Mr. Taylor's head. But it was too late. His head came down for a final blow, the sound sickening as bone and skin tore. His forehead broke away from the rest of his skull, cracked and oozing. His hair was tinted pink from the blood and just under the cracks the deep wrinkles of brain were visible.

I wanted to puke. I wanted to run. I wanted to do anything other than sit there. I felt her hands on me. They were cold, nearly icy to the touch. She pulled me from my seat and carried me to the door. Bits of blood and skin stained her hands. She left some on my shirt when she let go.

My ears rang. I felt my eyes grow heavier, my head splitting apart at the edges. *This isn't real.*

I laughed at the thought. The sound rushed past my lips before I could catch it. My classmates looked at me in tear-stricken disgust. Many of them were screaming, wailing from the traumatizing vision they were just subjected to. Jake was quiet for the first time since I'd moved here. A smile tugged at my lips.

"She did it!"

Everyone turned to look at me. Their wet eyes and red noses were like a sea of pain.

"Look what she did to Ivy and Autumn!" Another chimed in.

"That's enough!" Ms. Vera snapped. She pushed me forward, placing me on the curb as far away from them as she could. "I'm going to call your dad to come get you," Ms. Vera patted me on the shoulder.

I almost missed it. The first time my eyes glanced over her arms I hadn't noticed. Now that we were in brighter light outside, I could see them.

Deep black and yellow bruises covered her arms. Black veins stretched from one another spreading across her body like an intricate latticed spiderweb. *Impossible.*

Was it? I felt my stomach churn. That sickly feeling of dread pooled in my bones as fear sank a knife into my stomach. She looked just like her. The way she did in the beginning at least. I recognized them immediately. The yellowing of her teeth, the thinning hair, and the all too familiar bruises. Whatever got to Mom, it had gotten to Ms. Vera.

It was spreading.

Fifteen

"Farmers are outraged at the sudden rise in locusts sweeping through the region," The newswoman was pretty and her voice was smooth. Her long dark hair was tucked behind her ear. "This season's locusts are leaving behind stripped fields and destroyed land. Officials continue to claim the situation is under control, but farmers are uniting, stating the damage is already too significant and fear long-term economic consequences."

The TV cut to farmers lining the streets with their families. Everyone held signs marked with rushed hand painted designs and words. Some read *'Save Our Farms'*, *'No Crops, No Food, No Future'*, and another *'Fields Feed Families'*.

They didn't look sad. They looked angry, tired, and worn. Their fists rose in the air as they chanted. The camera shifted focus. A tall and burly man stood next to an interviewer. They were complete opposites. The interviewer wore a nice suit, and his hair was combed with gel. The farmer wore stained overalls and a flannel beneath it. His beard was scruffy and his hair rough.

"I'm Carlos Cantu coming at you live from the protest in downtown at the square," He glanced behind him as the crowd grew louder. "I'm here with Hugh Smith, a local farmer. What do you have to say about the situation?"

Hugh leaned toward the microphone, his large figure towering over the other man. "The situation is completely out of control. These locusts are like nothin' we've ever seen before."

"What makes you say that?"

"They don't die," Hugh threw his hands in defeat. "We've tried every safe pest control we could think of. I pride myself on my farm bein' organic, but that's not lookin' like I'll get to keep that title. It's just...you kill one a' 'em you get ten more. The county is lyin' to you. We ain't got this under control. There's no crops and no food. We're going to star-"

The camera cut back to the newswoman. "Well, there you have it. We'll keep you updated on the latest developments of this story. For now, this is Kayla Baker, reminding you stay safe and good night."

A commercial for cereal began to play. The colors were loud and aggressive. I turned to look at Dad. He looked exhausted. His eyes were dark and his look unkempt. This seemed to be his usual look recently.

Normally his hair was combed and styled, his face clean-shaven and his clothes without wrinkles. Today his hair hung in front of his eyes, greasy and tangled, a five o'clock shadow covered his chin, and he wore sweats for the first time in my life. He took a sip of coffee, his eyes reading across the screen of his laptop lazily.

"There's food in the fridge," He wouldn't look at me. "For when you get hungry."

I stayed silent for a bit. The sound of the commercials filling the void. He cleared his throat as he stood, disappearing into the kitchen.

"No blanket fort?"

"We can build one when I get back." He replied curtly.

Silence filled the air between us. I couldn't see him, but I knew he was preparing to leave. I knew he was filling a travel cup with fresh coffee, and I knew he wasn't going to care. I watched the commercial on the TV the music blaring through the speakers.

"Why can't you fix her?"

Silence.

"Dad," I called. It was a few moments before he came around the corner.

"What?" His tone was strained. He leaned against the wall with his shoulder.

"Why can't you fix her?" I repeated.

He sighed, crossing his arms. "Because I just can't."

"You haven't even tried."

"There is nothing to try, Petra," He ran a hand down his face.

"You could take her to your work," My eyes turned back to the TV. A new commercial, but this time for soap.

"I'm not going to do that."

"Why not?"

"Because..." His voice trailed off as he ran a hand through his hair. "Because she's already gotten better, hasn't she?"

That was a lie. Mom hadn't gotten better. She'd only hidden herself. She had been neatly tucked away in the main bedroom for over a week, and Dad seemed to be hoping she would stay that way. He just didn't want to deal with it.

"She's getting better, I promise," He sounded as if he were trying to convince himself. "I don't think this sickness is something the hospital can help. But I know someone who might."

"Another doctor?"

"No, but I promise it'll be fine. Mom will be fine," I turned back to him. He smiled. It was a grim and tired smile at best. Something between sorrow and guilt.

"You're a doctor."

"I know."

"You don't love her, do you?"

"That's enough," He suddenly moved, grabbing his coat and keys. "I'm heading out for a shift. Don't try to stay up."

He swung the door wide. "And make sure to brush your teeth."

I bit my tongue as the door slammed shut. He wasn't going to the hospital, nor to work. At least not dressed like that. I could feel the burn of anger spreading across my veins, raging like a wildfire as it tore through my lungs and throat.

I let out a sigh. I wanted to break everything in the room. To slam the TV on the ground and fling the coffee table across the room, but I knew I'd just get in trouble when he got back. I felt the familiar sting of tears in my eyes and lump in my throat. My hands shook and my breathing felt impossible to control. Alarms were blaring in my ears as my pulse grew louder and louder.

Then my eyes caught it. Dad's laptop. He had left it open on the dining room table. The dull blue glow from its screen suspending the shadows behind it. My eyes glanced above me, listening.

It was quiet, like it had been. No movement. No groaning of the floorboards. I silently made my way to it, climbing onto the chair.

The computer showed a picture of a forest on the screen. The time showing in large white block numbers. I looked at the stairs once more. Nothing. Just empty shadows and yellow light with the occasional white flash from the TV.

I clicked the mouse pad. The screen opening to a web page. My brow furrowed as I recognized the image on the screen.

The medallion.

The same ugly metallic disk with the same edges lined with foliage, and the head of the lion in the center with alternating horse and goat legs. I felt my stomach churn. My fingers scrolled down the page, my eyes scouring every word.

It seemed like the medallion belonged to Buer. A demon described as a Great President of Hell. He often appears as a lion's head with multiple goat and horse legs to walk in every direction. Then my heart fell to my stomach. There it was. The word Mr. Taylor had repeated.

Sagittarius. Buer appears when the Sun is in Sagittarius. The image of Mr. Taylor's mangled face consistently connecting with the table flashed against my eyes. The static began to grow louder in my ears. The hellish chorus grew into a deeper chant until it filled my ears, making it impossible to read. Once an angel of God, Buer fell when he joined Lucifer's rebellion. I felt sick, bile rising in my throat.

THUMP.

I jumped, electricity running through my bones. I turned to the stairs. The static in my ears was gone. I waited, holding my breath. After a moment, there wasn't any other noise.

I got up from the table and slowly made my way over to the base of the stairs. I put a hand on the railing. The wood was smooth and cold against my skin. Cautiously, I took one step...then another. Nothing but darkness greeted me. My ears felt like they were ringing. The silence felt impossibly quiet. I was halfway up, my fingers shaking in anticipation.

My heart stopped. I felt my body freeze. She was there. In the darkness, just barely visible. Her pale face morphing behind the wall of shadows. The rest of her body was only a silhouette. Her eyes we still slightly reflective. She smiled. Each side of her lips tipped upwards in slow motion, her teeth glinted faintly.

"M-Mo-Mom?"

She lunged. I couldn't move fast enough. My feet got tied up as I panicked, tripping over myself, my hand slipped from the railing as I tried desperately to escape. The world spun, lights and colors mixing. My body crumpled against the wood of the stairs, different body parts slamming into the wall and railing.

I came to a halt against the wall at the bottom of the stairs. My head felt warm and fuzzy. I sucked in a breath, pain shooting through me. Tears ran down my cheeks as I tried to move. My body felt oddly disconnected. I tried to lift my right arm, but my fingers only twitched and my left leg shifted. I let out a pained cry. It hurt. It hurt *so* much.

My eyes wandered along the stairs. Mom stood there. Halfway down. Her expression was blank. I half expected her to run to me, to cradle me in her arms.

"M-Mom," My voice was barely audible. "*Mom.*"

She didn't move.

"*Help...p-please*," I croaked out the words in a raspy and grating whisper as the taste of iron filled my mouth. I thought she'd snap out of it.

I hoped she'd apologize for everything she'd done. I hoped she'd hold me to take the pain away. I hoped she'd be like before and sing to me while she called Dad.

Tears mixed with snot along my face and lip. The pain lighting up in agonizing flames. My vision grew fuzzy around the edges. The pain was too much, it made my heart hurt.

I hoped my Mom would come back.

The Mom I begrudgingly attended fossil museums with. The Mom who cooked bland meals and made Dad complain. The Mom who uprooted our entire lives to pursue her passion. The Mom who would buy me ice cream if so much as a thorn poked me outside. The Mom who insisted on kissing me every time I got home from school. The Mom who tucked me in during thunderstorms and let me sleep next to her when I had nightmares.

Instead, I just had to watch as she turned away and walked back up the stairs into the dark. *My* Mom was never coming back.

Sixteen

"Stop talking."

"You left her there by herself?"

"I said to stop talking."

"She's your daughter, James."

"Can you leave?"

"Are you serious right now?"

"I don't want to talk to you and you're not welcome here."

My eyes flitted open but immediately closed against the immensely bright light. As my eyes adjusted to the white, fluorescent lights I could make out the white walls and white sheets. It smelled like cleaning supplies and old linen. I was in a hospital.

"James, just tell me what's going on," Ms. Vera. I recognized her voice now. "You owe that much to me at least."

"I don't owe you shit," Dad. His tone was cruel. "You knew what you were getting into. It was no strings attached."

Ms. Vera scoffed. "Yeah, that was until you gave me whatever STD you gave your wife."

"Leave," His spoke through gritted teeth. "I never want to see you again. You disgust me."

"Is this what you do with every woman?" Her voice was filled with venom. "You only like them when they're pretty but the minute, they start to get sick you chuck them away?"

"No-"

"It's what you did to your wife and now me-"

"Don't talk about my wife."

There was a tension-filled pause that blanketed the air.

"I want to make sure she's okay," Her voice was a whisper. "The kids at school are scared of her."

"I shouldn't have left," He choked on the words. "I just can't stay there. Not with what's happening."

"I know," Ms. Vera placed a hand on his shoulder. He pulled away.

"You don't," He pinched the bridge of his nose before running his hands through his hair. "You will never understand."

I opened my eyes fully, turning my head to face them at the right end of the bed.

"Petra," Ms. Vera sounded shocked. She rushed over to my side. "Sweety how are you feeling?" She cooed over me, tucking a stray strand of hair behind my ear.

I shrugged. My body felt sore and numb. I looked down at my arms, they were riddled with dark purple bruises, long semi-transparent black veins climbing around my arms like spider webs. My throat felt like sandpaper as I swallowed.

"Just get some rest, kid," Dad moved toward me, all but shoving Ms. Vera out of the way. She looked like she wanted to say something but decided against it. "Everything is going to be fine."

A doctor stepped through the door swiftly moving around to the left side of the room. Two police officers followed suit and a woman with a clipboard in hand.

"Dr. Craven, this is Mrs. Spinell," The man had a higher pitched voice. "She and the officers are here to speak with Petra."

"Why?" Dad stepped forward.

"Sir, we don't want to cause any trouble," Mrs. Spinell was pretty. Her short red hair was cropped in a sleek bob just below her jawline. Her eyes were the color of freshly rained on grass, that dark and soft kind of green. "We just need to speak with her for a few minutes. It won't take any time at all."

"You have no reason to talk with her," Dad gripped at the bed sheets, balling them into his fist.

"Actually, they do," The doctor chimed in nervously. "Look Dr. Craven, *James*, you know the rules. We see something we have to report it."

"You reported *me*?"

"It's not anything personal, just policy," The doctor fidgeted with his stethoscope. "A child 'falling down the stairs' and coming in with an erratic parent?"

"You're calling me erratic?" Dad looked betrayed.

"Please Mr. Craven, if nothing has happened you don't have anything to worry about," Mrs. Spinell took a step forward, her high heel clicking on the ground.

"You're going to have something to worry about in a second," Dad stepped up to her angrily, the two officers pushed forward.

"Alright, let's go outside and take a break," One of them spoke gruffly.

"Don't touch me!" Dad shoved one of them back. The other grabbed him by the shirt. "Not in front of my kid!"

"Let's go Mr. Craven," They each grabbed at his arms and shoulders dragging him from the room.

"Petra!" Dad craned his neck to face me, his eyes wild. "Petra!"

The door closed. Ms. Vera had tears in her eyes, the doctor looked frazzled and Mrs. Spinell sighed.

"I'm sorry, but the two of you have to leave as well," Her voice was calm.

"Right sorry," The doctor rushed hurriedly out the door, followed by Ms. Vera.

"Hi Petra," Mrs. Spinell pulled a chair over to the side of the bed. "I'm not here to harm you, and I'm sorry about what just happened. I just want to ask a few questions, is that okay?"

She smelled nice, like blooming lilies. Mom used to buy a lot of flowers before we moved. I think lilies were her favorite.

"Okay," My voice was scratchy and dry and my lips were chapped. I bit at them.

"Here," She pulled a small water bottle from her purse. "Does that feel better?"

I drank it hungrily. My thirst felt impossible to quench. It was rooted so deep into my bones I was barely breathing as I gulped the water down. Once I'd chugged the bottle, she took it from my hands, tossing it into the small trashcan by my bedside.

"You ready for some questions?" She smiled with lipstick smudged across her front teeth. I nodded.

"Let's start with what happened and how did it happen?"

"I fell down the stairs at home," I watched her expression, but it didn't change. She held the same smile if only a little smaller.

"Was anyone home with you?"

"Mom was home," She nodded at my response.

"And your Dad? Where was he?"

"I don't know."

"Does he often leave at night?"

"He works here, so sometimes he works extra," I could hear the wavering of my own voice.

"Was it just you and your mom at home?"

"Yeah."

"Did she make you fall down the stairs?"

Mom lunging at me flashed through my mind. I hesitated. *Would she do something about Mom?* I doubted it.

"No," The word came out softly as if I wasn't confident in my answer. She only nodded, her lips pursed. She knew I was lying.

"Do you feel safe at home?"

I thought about the last few weeks. *Is home safe?*

Not in the slightest. Mom was sick and acted really strange. Dad was never home to deal with it or protect me. During the bonfire I really thought I was going to die.

The silence must have lasted for a while. She cleared her throat. "Petra, you can be honest with me."

My eyes wandered to the door. Dad had struggled against the officers. He was upset. Maybe he did truly care in his own way. Maybe he was worried.

"I'm safe at home," I could tell she didn't like that answer. Her brow furrowed and she sucked in her cheeks. She marked a few things on her clipboard.

"Do you think you'll get hurt again?"

Yes. "No."

"What do you do when you're at home? Do you and your mom hang out?" She gave a small smile.

"No," I shook my head. "Sometimes we would go dig outside, but normally I just watch TV. Mom is sick."

"Your mom is sick? How so?"

"She's lost a lot of her hair and doesn't come out of her room anymore," I shrugged. "She's got bruises and doesn't eat either. She's been acting kind of weird at night."

"Weird at night how?"

I bit at my lip. "I don't know. She's just weird. She makes weird noises and does weird things."

"What weird things? Give me an example," She leaned forward.

"She tried to break into my room one night, um, and she was naked outside a few nights ago," I kept my eyes on hers, waiting for any sort of slip of emotion, but none came. She just nodded along.

"Does your dad usually come get your mom when she does these things?"

I shook my head. "No, he's usually not home."

"That's right. I understand," The scratching of her pen against the papers was loud amid the small moment of silence. "Do you feel like you're taken care of at home?"

"I think so."

"Alright," She smiled, standing and clicking her pen away. She placed the clipboard under her arm and left the room. I could hear muffled voices through the door but couldn't quite discern what was being said.

After what seemed like several minutes the doctor came back in with Dad.

"Let's go," Dad threw the blanket off my legs, the cold of the air sending a shock through me. Goosebumps raised on my skin immediately.

"James, give her a moment-"

"I'm not giving you bastards any more moments. You reported me. We're supposed to be friends Nicholas," Dad looked exhausted. Large heavy bags of puffy skin sat under his bloodshot eyes, his stubble was longer. He was still in those sweats from before, stained and wrinkled.

"James please-"

"Come on Petra, get up," He grabbed me by the wrist and jerked me out of the bed. It hurt. My skin twisted in his hand.

"James!" Dad rushed us down the hall, ignoring the other doctor and past the two officers who stood talking with Mrs. Spinell. They eyed us as Dad practically drug me through the doors.

"Hey, Mr. Craven," The one with tattoos along his forearms spoke up, waving a hand at us. "Let me speak to you a moment."

"Absolutely not," Dad continued down the sidewalk heading to the parking lot.

"Mr. Craven!" The cop ran after us.

"Leave us alone," Dad unlocked the car pulling the passenger door open and pushing me inside. "Buckle up."

A hand stopped the door from shutting. "Mr. Craven."

"What do you want? Didn't you have enough? Dragging me out of the room where my daughter was?"

"Mr. Craven I assure you we meant no harm," The officer gave a wry smile. "I just wanted to give this to you."

Dad took the card from his hand. "What's this?"

"It's the home I built for people like my mother. For early onset dementia," The officer glanced at me. "It's a real good place sir. I work there and still run the place. It's my second job."

"Why're you giving me this?"

"Well per our conversation with Mrs. Spinell over there I just figured it might be of some help."

"Well, it's not," Dad shoved the card into his pocket before hurriedly moving to the driver side.

"That's my number on the card," The officer met my eyes. "If you ever need to reach me, just give that number a call."

"We won't be, thanks," With that Dad slammed the door shut and put the keys in the ignition. The officer closed my door and stepped back. His eyes looked sad as he watched us pull away.

I wondered if I'd ever see him again. Maybe if Mom did act strange again, I could call him. I'd just have to get the card from Dad, which I doubt he'd let me have it.

Seventeen

Every fiber of my muscles felt like it had been torn apart. The soreness had seeped so deeply through my muscles it had drenched and sagged my bones. My mind felt as if it was fraying at the seams. My eyes burned and my throat was dry. I tilted my head.

Dad had been quiet since we got back. He had driven far over the speed limit to get home, acting crazy. He had mumbled a lot of explicit words under his breath but nothing worth listening to. At the moment, he was pacing back and forth through the kitchen, running his hands through his hair that was now greased with sweat.

My eyes kept returning to the stairs. The remnants from last night still stained the wood. Blood streaked across the floor and walls, not enough to look like a crime scene but just enough to be a warning. I looked back at my water on the coffee table. Small rivulets of water trailed the side of the glass. The water pooled along the base, running into the grooves of the wood.

My eyes continued to wander, stalling on the mold on the ceiling. It seemed to have dried a bit since I last looked at it, but it had spread across the back wall. My gaze continued to follow the mold, then my brow furrowed. Small fungus and vines pushed through the flooring. My eyes began to scour everything they could reach. They were everywhere. The small leaves were tucked away in the shadows, hiding in plain sight. I couldn't believe I hadn't noticed this earlier. How long have they been there? There were hundreds of them, crawling along the floor in awkward patterns, avoiding foot traffic and furniture.

"I have to go," Dad grabbed his coat and keys once more. He rushed to put his shoes on, struggling with the laces as his hands shook. "Stay downstairs. If something happens-"

He cut himself off, hands scrambling into his pockets. He pulled out the wrinkled card the officer had handed him earlier. "Call this number if something happens."

He placed it in my hand. My eyes moved to look at the old home phone. It was covered in a pile of dust and old cobwebs, but its dull screen still shined in the dim light.

"Okay."

"Okay?" Dad grabbed me by the shoulders. "I'll be right back. Just give me a few minutes. If something happens...run."

And with that he sped out the door. I listened as his car engine started, and the tires peeled out of the driveway. I was alone in the house...*again*.

I carefully lay down on the couch. My muscles were stiff and all my joints were swollen. I reached a hand up to feel the bandage on my head. I winced as I felt the small lumps where the stitches were. I looked down at my arms. The bruises had spread and long black veins traced lattice-like paths between each. The bruises had grown into rich purples and deep yellows.

Would my hair start falling out too? Would I start acting strange at night? Would I dance around a fire with sheep?

I shuddered at the thought. Instead of worrying about it any longer, I pulled a blanket over me. I was tired, my body worn. Exhaustion crept over me, weighing on me as sleep tugged at my eyes. My eyelids lulled closed as my mind slipped away.

A muffled sound woke me up. My ears could barely pick it up, but somehow it felt familiar. I kept my eyes closed, trying to focus on just the sound. It grew louder, encompassing my ears in its entirety. A small *tick, tick, tick.* I felt my blood run cold.

I sat up. *The medallion.*

Where was it? I hadn't seen it since in a while. The lion head gleaming in gold flashed against my mind. Its empty stare greedy. I tried to listen harder, but it had already stopped.

The sound of a car in the driveway tore my attention to the door. It was still dark outside so I couldn't have been asleep for long. The car hadn't shut off, which was odd if it were Dad. I waited to hear movement above me but was greeted with silence.

Making my way to the door I could see from the window a cop car sitting in the driveway. The car was old and mud covered the tires. I squinted, trying to see better, as a familiar figure stepped from the vehicle. I opened the door just as a dog stepped from the car to sit next to the man.

"Kiddo?" His gruff voice carried easily over the quiet night air.

"Hi," I stepped out of the house.

"How're you feeling?" His eyes searched the area around him.

"I'm okay."

"I'm sorry, I didn't mean to wake you up kiddo," The dog whined nervously. "Where's your dad at?"

I shrugged.

"Alright," He wiped a hand across his brow. "Where's your mom at?"

"Right here."

My heart lurched. I could feel the color drain from my face as I turned to see her. She stood in the doorway with a hand on her hip and smile across her lips. Something was wrong. Something was horribly wrong. Mom looked like *Mom*. The Mom I knew from before. Her hair was neatly tied back into a bun and was no longer greasy and falling out. Her teeth were perfectly pearly white, and her gums weren't filled with black sludge. There were no bruises on her skin or sickly veins to match mine. She looked normal, but that's what made it feel worse... Her frame was still thin, but not to the point of looking sickly. She wore cargo pants and a simple graphic tee.

"What can I do for you officer?" She smiled that same almost too wide grin.

"Oh nothing, I was just checking on your kid here," The officer was jerked by the arm as his dog began to lunge. Its shrill and angered barks were aimed at Mom. Saliva frothed at its mouth as it continued to pull and snap its teeth in the air as its two front paws lifted from the ground.

"I'm so sorry, he normally doesn't act like this," The officer gave a sheepish grin before opening his car door and putting the dog away.

"Sorry, just remind me why you're trespassing on my property at this time of night?" Mom checked her watch before crossing her arms. She annoyedly tapped her left foot.

"I'm sorry ma'am I didn't mean to bother," The officer let out a small laugh. "I just wanted to check on the kiddo and make sure she was doing alright after your husband rushed her out of the hospital."

"Right, well she's doing just fine," Mom placed a hand on my shoulder. I pulled away just as a slight reflective glint hit her eyes. "But you really shouldn't have come here."

"Pardon?"

"You're a good person so don't take it too hard," She stepped toward the officer closing the distance. "But not everyone can be saved."

She closed the distance fast grabbing the officer by the throat, digging her fingers beneath his skin. She tore a handful of flesh as blood poured from the wound. Her jaw unhinged, opening wider than humanely possible. My body wouldn't move. I couldn't breathe. My lungs burned and my pulse pounded in my ears.

The officers arms grabbed and pushed at her but she wouldn't budge, her grip too strong as her hands tore at his chest. Her fingers tore through muscle and bone. She bit down on his head with a sickening crunch rending the flesh from his face as she ate away nearly half his skull. The officer let out a gurgled scream and grabbed at her arms, but it was no use. Blood splattered on the ground, mangled flesh hanging haphazardly as Mom went in for another bite.

My body finally reacted. *Run.* I tore across the driveway, my feet slipping as they met with dead leaves in the yard. I didn't look back. The wet screams of the officer echoed through my ears as I ran. I ran for my life. Sprinting toward the sheep, vaulting over the fence, but my shirt caught and I crashed to the ground. I felt warmth spread along my brow, my hand reached up. Blood covered my fingers. I stood, a bit dizzy.

The sheep only stared at me at first, but then they charged. The sheep bit at any part of me they could reach. Their teeth weren't sharp, but they hurt just the same. They pinched at my skin and clothes, just barely breaking through leaving small trails of blood. I tried to push past them, moving as fast as I could.

I made my way to the shed throwing the door open and shutting it behind me. There wasn't any light in the shed. Complete darkness enveloped me as I tried to catch my breath. I felt around in the dark as I had so many times before. My hands grazed across a ledge. I grimaced as I began to pull myself up. My body screamed in agony, lighting up across every one of my muscles. It took everything in me to not scream in pain.

Once on top of the shelf, I squeezed myself behind the small square hay bales at the back wall. It was mostly silent.

The hay made my eyes watery and my nose itch. I don't know how long I held my breath, but I refused to breathe, choosing to listen for any movement.

Any crumbling of the leaves made my heart skip a beat. *It's the sheep.* I would tell myself. My lungs burned and my body felt heavy. The hay stabbed through my clothes and dug into my skin. I held still.

My ears pricked up at the subtle sound of a car engine and tires on concrete. I waited, hearing the door open and close, the dog barking in the other car, and the sound of panicked shuffling.

"Petra!" Dad was home. His voice rang clear even through the darkened shed. I didn't move at first, wanting to be sure it was him. "Petra! Where are you?"

I don't know what kept me in my hiding spot. Maybe it was all the nights before. Maybe it was how Mom seemed to change herself so easily. Maybe it was that I didn't believe Dad would ever come back for me.

"Petra! Please!" His voice was closer now, guilt ridden and gritty. "Petra! Shit!"

I could hear the movement of hooves. Dad had stepped into the fray. The sheep probably nipped at him like they did me. My stomach churned as the shed door began to pull open, the light from the backside of the house flooding in.

The person was shrouded in shadow. Their face was completely obscured. I held my breath as they drew closer, their hands fumbling around in the dark. They grabbed at the hay I laid behind pulling it away from the wall.

"Petra?" The light hit his face just right and his eyes didn't reflect. It was Dad. The fear in his eyes was evident. His hair was a mess. "Come here."

I crawled to his outstretched arms, letting him pull me down from the shelf. He rushed out of the shed, hugging me tight to his chest. I watched over his shoulder as the sheep bit at his legs and pants. Their teeth tore through the denim, drawing blood, but he never slowed, clearing the fence and rushing to the driveway.

He put me down. "Where is your mother?"

"I don't know."

He hung his head, swiping his hand through his hair. He sucked in a breath. "You ran."

"Yeah."

"Good job," He gave a wry smile. "You did good. I'm proud of you. You kept yourself safe."

"I did." I could feel tears welling behind my eyes. I knew the body of the officer was right behind me, his dog wailing in the car still.

"What happened? Did you call him?"

"No," I shook my head. "He just showed up. Mom came outside and-"

"Okay," He pursed his lips. "It's alright."

My eyes wandered past Dad who sat thinking of what to do next. The front door sat ajar. The crack that led into the house was devoid of any light. Instead, it seemed to draw it in and strangle it. Shadows moved and crept past eyeing the both of us, waiting for us to enter.

"You did so good, I'm so proud of you," Dad hugged me close. He nearly squeezed all the air out of my lungs. As he pulled me away, I could see tears pooling in his eyes. He wiped the hair out of my face. "What happened to your head?"

"I fell."

He laughed a bit at my response. "Let's get out of here, yeah?"

I nodded. He opened the driver side door to his car, and I crawled over the center console into the passenger seat. He sat in the car and pulled the door closed. As he reached for the ignition his face dropped. He began to look around the car, pulling up the center console, and pulling down the sun visor.

"Where are the keys?" He began frantically patting his pockets. "Do you see them?"

I looked around, but there was nothing. "No."

"*Fuck*," He punched the steering wheel. His eyes fell on the review mirror. "The cop. Wait here."

Dad rushed out of the car. I watched from the side mirror as he patted down the officer's body. The dog was still howling in the car. Dad pulled on the officer's car door, hunting through the two front seats. He shook his head coming back to the driver's side of his car.

"There aren't any keys," He ran a hand through his hair a few times. My eyes flitted to the open door of the house.

"Do you think she has them?" I asked. Dad's eyes followed my gaze.

"Yeah, probably," His expression was grim and his jaw tightened. "Stay in here. Don't go inside after me for any reason. Do you understand?"

I nodded.

"If I don't come back out in thirty minutes, run. Run to the neighbors or anywhere. Just don't stay here," He stood up straight. "I love you kid."

"I love you too Dad," The words barely pushed over the lump in my throat. If he went in there he wasn't going to come out. I could feel it deep in my heart. Dread poured its way through my veins and bones making me lightheaded. I watched in anticipation, holding my breath, as he crossed the threshold of the house.

It felt like forever. Little bugs fluttered on tiny wings through the front light of the house. Their shadows danced along the wall and door. The rest of the world remained quiet. No lights came on in the house. No sound echoed through the night as the dog had stopped barking long ago. I couldn't tell how much time had passed. The car was off, so the clock didn't display on the dash. I hadn't moved an inch since he went through the door, my muscles growing stiff.

He told me to run, but I still held hope that he would come out of the house. That he'd have his keys in hand and drive us as far away as possible.

A hand slid from the shadows of the door. It was ghostly white, pushing through the darkness like a thick cloud. Its shadow danced across the ground as its fingers stretched into a wave. It beckoned me forward before slipping back into the dark.

Dad said not to move, but I found my fingers reaching for the door handle. It popped open freely, my feet stepping onto the cool concrete of the driveway. I stepped to the front of the car before looking behind me.

The officer's mangled corpse lay splayed across the ground. I could feel bile rise in my throat at the sight. His skin was hanging in bloodied chunks, his bones jutting out of his face at odd angles, what was left of them anyway. A pool of blood circled around him in a near perfect halo. I shuddered.

My attention turned back to the door. The door was wide open now, the darkness absorbing any light that came near it. I took a tentative step forward. I could feel my pulse in my ears. I took another step forward. Then another.

I stood at the threshold of the door. It was too dark to see inside. I poked my head in, peering around at the living room and kitchen. Dad's feet flashed up the stairs.

"Dad?"

Silence.

The wood beneath my feet groaned in quiet warning as my hand trailed the railing. I could feel the shaking of my hands and legs, but I continued. My throat felt dry and my stomach churned until I felt the air in my lungs dissipate. Each step was tortuous. I didn't want to continue, but my body marched on, pushing me forward, each foot rising to the next step.

At the top it was quiet. The silence ringing through my ears. The doors were all closed except for one. My parent's bedroom hung open in surrender.

I made my way forward. Small whispers filtered through the air, drowning against the sound of my footsteps. They were quiet, unintelligible. As I moved closer, they grew louder, turning into static as their voices overlapped. The chorus poured into my mind like a parasitic rot. It pulled at the edges of my vision and tore through my mind like a fire. The voices danced around the smallest parts of my mind, jumping through my thoughts and memories like a swarm of locusts. It pulled at me like a lullaby threatening to take over.

"Petra."

I jolted. Fear laced my bones in ice. Mom stood in front of me. Her sickly figure back. Her hair was mostly gone, her teeth rotted, and her eyes almost completely black.

"Mom?" This couldn't be real. It couldn't be. She was better. She looked better when she hurt the officer. She was *better*.

"Oh darling, your mother isn't here," She smiled, too wide and too crooked. "But I know where she is." Her voice grew louder. The chanting in my ears slowly pulling its long fingers out of my mind, releasing its grasp.

"You kn-know w-where she is?"

"Of course I do," Her voice grew deeper. "I've been keeping her safe."

"Safe?"

She nodded. My entire body trembled. I wanted to run. Every fiber of my soul wanted me to run. "I can bring her back."

"You can?" I felt my heart jump at the idea.

"And I can do so much more, my dear," She pulled a stray hair away from my ear, twirling it around her fingers. Her nails were covered in dirt.

"Can I have my Mom back now?" My voice wavered. *Was this it*?

"Of course," She tucked the hair away. "You want both of them back right?"

"Both?" I felt my brow furrow. Movement caught the corner of my eye. Dad sat in the corner of the room. His keys tucked against his palm. He looked like he was sleeping. I felt a hand pull my chin.

"Both of them," Mom was closer now. "They haven't been the same since you moved. Mom and Dad were growing apart. They fought so much, didn't they?"

"They did," I glanced at Dad.

"They did," She almost sang the words. "I am a great healer. Did you know that?"

My mind thought of the words I read on Dad's laptop. I slowly nodded.

"Good, smart girl," She cupped my face. "I can give you what you've always wanted. I can cure them of all their ailments."

She wiped a thumb across my cheek. Had I been crying? I couldn't tell.

"You could have it all," Her smile grew wider. "No more mom going thump in the night. No more dad getting angry or leaving. No more bullies or homework or school."

"You can really do that?" I couldn't feel my legs anymore. My stomach felt like its contents were boiling over.

"I absolutely can," She placed her hands on my shoulder as she knelt. "I can heal the illness of man. But you must help me."

She clutched my right hand close to her heart. The chorus of whispers began again faintly. The house felt colder somehow. My arms prickled and the hair on the back of my neck pricked up. It felt like thousands of eyes were on us, but it was just me and her.

"I just need something from you," Her voice echoed through my ears in a way that didn't make sense. "Just tell me you're mine."

"What?" My eyes snapped to hers.

"Resign your soul to me and you'll have everything," She gripped my hand tighter. "The illness of man will be gone, and you'll be safe with your parents. As if none of this ever happened."

My heart was loud against my chest. Something felt wrong. I glanced at Dad, his eyes were still shut. I could save him. I could save all of us. I could bring them back to before.

"O-okay."

"Yes, my dear," She put her lips by ear. Her voice grew quiet. "Say these words."

Words I didn't understand in a language I didn't recognize poured from her mouth. I felt my breath stutter through my lungs, my heart skipping as my head pounded. The echoes of voices in the static intensified. The voices twisting and turning until they braided themselves into one coherent piece. They flowed along Mom's voice tugging at one another until the braid smoothed out.

I repeated the words. My ears were bleeding, my skull crushing in as the words spilled from my lips. They felt hot as they skipped across my tongue. When I finished, the static instantly stopped, my vision clear.

Mom laughed as she pulled away. The laugh rippled up from her stomach and stretched across the air. The laugh transformed into something ugly as it clawed at her lungs and throat. It turned my blood cold.

"Oh child," Her voice morphed, several voices collapsing over one another. "I'm so proud of you."

Long strands of sinew burst through her skin. Her flesh tore in jagged edges. She laughed once more, cackling in an unholy manner. I fell to the floor as her mouth gaped open her teeth shattering as the head of a lion pushed out of her throat. Her face folded in on itself, the bones crunching and snapping. Her arms tore away, falling to the ground in a spray of blood.

Screams tore through me. I couldn't hold it in any longer. Why was this happening? What is going on? I thought I did everything right! I thought I was helping!

"I want my Mom!" I screamed. "I want my Dad!" And it was true. God was it so true! I would give anything for them to be holding me. I would give anything to go back in time before that day. Before Mom, *my* Mom, ever touched that stupid medallion.

"And you'll join them," Legs burst through her back and sides. They were covered in thick blood and black veins pulsing through their skin. The fur was dampened and rough, the hooves shining in the dim light of the moon. Three horse legs and three goat legs. *Buer.*

I screamed again. The taste of iron filled my mouth as the animalistic noise tore from my throat. Hot tears raced down my cheeks. My body felt like it was on fire again. The flames traced my skin and licked at my guts leaving nothing but embers and ash in its wake.

I was suddenly lying in the forest. I was panting, drinking in the cool, fresh air. The sky was a powdery blue. The sun was rising. It was morning. My breathing slowed. The grass was dewy, the moisture soaking through the back of my shirt and pants.

I'm tired. My body was sore and stiff. My fingers were buried in the dirt. It felt good to lay down. The dirt was cold and the grass was soft. Birds sang and flew through the air, the sound of their wings drifting in every direction. It smelled like it had rained or was going to. I smiled as my eyes grew heavy. Sleep wrapped its hands around my arms, coiling itself along my entire body. It blanketed me in comfort, rendering my arms immobile. I tried to move my hands but it grew tighter, cutting off the circulation to my fingers and toes. I gasped.

My eyes flew open. Vines writhed along my skin, digging themselves deeper and deeper. I felt a scream tear through my throat as thorns tunneled into my arms and legs The vines were still growing, stretching across my throat, chest, and face.

Why?

My skin tore. The skin ripping apart as the vines constricted further. They clamped down harder as I struggled against them. My arms began to sink, following my fingers below Earth's surface.

Why?

Dirt began to fall over my arms and neck. My legs were next, then my hips and chest. My face barely poked above the surface. I closed my mouth as it drew near. It already covered my ears, spilling into them. My hearing was gone. I couldn't hear my own screaming and crying. I could feel the snot and tears, but there was no noise. Nothing could be heard of my struggle. The dirt rose in the corner of my eyes. It fell into my nose and poured across my cheeks mixing with tears and snot. I was alone. Again.

God help me.

Acknowledgements

To the love of my life. The very person who never stopped believing in me. The person who continues to stand through every moment with me. The person who cheers me on in every corner and possesses my every thought. For every hour spent writing this book, there were countless more with rambling ideas patiently endured. I will forever be grateful to share all my book ideas with him forever.

To Skipper, Mags, and now Todd, for all the pets and playtime in between and all the many things knocked from my desk, I love you three.

About the Author

A writer by night and an engineer by day. Kaitlyn studied and graduated with her bachelor's degree in chemical engineering. Following a long day of work, she comes home to the little pitter-patter of paws upon the floor.

After dreaming incessantly of becoming an author, she finally took the leap. Each work of hers is nothing short of her heart poured onto the pages.

www.ingramcontent.com/pod-product-compliance
Lightning Source LLC
Chambersburg PA
CBHW010600310726
48969CB00009B/2507